GOOD 2 GO

CHILDHOOD SWEETHEARTS III

A Novel

JACOB SPEARS

Good 2 Go Publishing

Childhood Sweethearts 3
Written by Jacob Spears
Cover design: Davida Baldwin
Typesetter: Mychea
ISBN: 9781943686650

Copyright ©2016 Good2Go Publishing
Published 2016 by Good2Go Publishing
7311 W. Glass Lane • Laveen, AZ 85339
www.good2gopublishing.com
https://twitter.com/good2gobooks
G2G@good2gopublishing.com
www.facebook.com/good2gopublishing
www.instagram.com/good2gopublishing

Printed in the USA

CHILDHOOD SWEETHEARTS III

A Novel

JACOB SPEARS

DEDICATION

I would like to dedicate this book to a very rare and sincere friend—someone who is always there for me: Clifford Wallach. Thank you for being on my team and thank you for always being there.

ACKNOWLEDGEMENT

First and foremost, I want to acknowledge a very good man who has helped me a lot. Thank you L.T. Bettineschi. I'd also like to acknowledge the other old man, Sgt. Joseph. I'd like to give a shout out to my mom, Lenora Sarantos; my cousin, Eleah Huff; my Aunt Bertie; my brother, Chris Hopkins; and the best sister in the world, Amy McKinney.

Thanks also go to Eries Tisdale (aka Guru); Trayvon Jackson (aka Sue Rabbit); Nurse Tara; George Hamilton (aka Ham), Tovorres Alexander (aka TIC aka Lunatic); Deputies E. Spencer and S. Cranmer; Franklyn Neswick; Depado; Nurse Karen; Deputy Young (Yes, Young, you are in here!); Tate; Elisa and Mary; and the best-looking is you, Mrs. Tolley.

I won't forget Deputy Hammond. Thank you for all the help and batteries. I'd also like to give a shout out to John Hetherington and Ray Brown. Last but not least, I want to thank all my fans and shout out to all my brothers and sisters who are locked up.

ONE

China was sitting at the poker table playing a card game called skin when she noticed a girl cheating.

"Bitch is cheating!" China exclaimed.

"Who you calling a bitch?"

"You!" China said, as she slapped the girl.

"Oh, it's on now, bitch!"

"Get to the room then," China ordered.

China headed to the room with the girl following her.

"I'm gonna teach you a lesson," the girl said, as she took a swing at China.

China sidestepped and punched the girl right in the nose. Blood shot out everywhere. The girl tried to tackle China and they both fell to the floor. China then flipped the girl off of her, climbed on top of her, and started punching the girl. Left, right, left, right. China continued to beat the shit out her until she felt someone punch her in the back three times. The pain was blinding. China reached behind her and felt warm wetness. Pulling her hand back and looking at it, it was covered in blood. The room started to spin.

China's last thought was that someone had stabbed her. Then her world went blank . . . dark . . . finished.

* * *

Smooth woke up the next morning and found Rebecca pacing the living room floor.

"What's wrong?" Smooth asked.

"You might want to sit down."

"Why?"

TWO

Pulling into the parking lot, Sue Rabbit saw Prince Guru leaning against his blacked-out Dodge Charger talking to two of their runners. Parking next to the Charger, Sue got out of the car and joined the other three.

"What's up, Sue?" Guru asked as he gave him dap.

"Can't call it. What's up with y'all?"

"Just trying to get that money," replied one of their runners, Mark.

"I feel that!" Sue turned to Guru.

How are you on product?" Sue asked.

"We good for now, but might need to re-up in a few hours."

"Just give me call," Sue said, giving everyone dap and heading back to his car.

Turning right out of the parking lot, Sue headed to Ronny's place. Halfway there, he saw a bunch of girls wearing two-piece bathing suits and washing cars. He decided to get his car washed, even though he just had it washed the day before. He pulled into the parking lot and four girls came over. Sue got out of his car to greet them.

"Hey, ladies! How much to get it washed?"

"We don't charge. We take donations. So, give whatever you want. It's all for a good cause," one of the girls added.

Looking at the four girls, he saw they were all good looking with nice bodies, but one girl in a red bathing suit stood out. She was absolutely beautiful and thick. Her breasts looked like they were fixing to pop out of her top.

"What are you taking donations for?" Sue asked.

"One our fellow cheerleaders was killed in a car wreck so we are taking donations for her family for funeral costs."

"So, you're all cheerleaders?"

"Yeah!" the thick one said.

"Well, here!" Sue said, handing over 10 $100 bills.

"This is $1,000!"

"I know. I hope it helps!"

"Well, let us get to work," one of them responded.

"Hey ma, can I holler at ya for a minute?" Sue asked the thick one.

"Yeah? What's up?"

"I was wondering if you'd like to go out tonight. You can pick where we go."

"Alright," she replied.

"How about 6:00 p.m.?"

"Sounds good," she answered

"Good! Then let me give you my phone number."

"Boy, does it look like I got anything to write down?"

"You're right! Sorry. Here, give me your number, and I will call you around 5:30."

After putting her phone number in his phone, she went and helped the other three girls wash his car.

"Damn! Shorty got it going on!" Sue said to himself.

THREE

66 Why do I need to sit down?" Smooth asked.

"I just think you should, 'cause I'm not sure how you'll react to what I gotta say," Rebecca replied.

"Alright," Smooth said, as he sat down.

"Now tell me!" he insisted.

"I'm not sure how to tell you," she said.

"Just spit it out!"

"Okay. I'm pregnant!"

"What?"

"I'm pregnant," Rebecca repeated.

Smooth sat there stunned.

"Well, say something!"

"Are you sure?"

"I took two different tests. So, yeah, I'm sure!"

Smooth stood up and walked over to her.

"I'm gonna be a dad!" Smooth said, as he kissed her forehead and wrapped his arms around her.

She started to cry.

"Why are you crying?"

"'Cause I'm happy. I thought for sure you'd be upset."

"I'm not upset," he responded.

"Well, there is one more major problem."

"What?" he asked.

"We got to tell China. How you think she's gonna take it?" she asked.

"Not sure, but don't tell her on the phone. I will tell her in person so I can see how she takes it."

* * *

Paco hung from a cherry picker begging for mercy.

"Please! Don't hurt me anymore. I'll tell ya anything," he begged.

"I gave you a chance," Spencer replied, as he grabbed a curling iron, which was connected to an extension cord.

"This might hurt a bit, but it will warm you up!" Spencer laughed.

Walking around behind Paco, Spencer shoved the curling iron up his ass and turned it on.

"This will be interesting," Spencer said, as Paco started screaming.

All of a sudden, he felt his phone vibrate. Looking at the display, he saw it was his sister.

"Hello?" he asked, as he answered.

"Hey bro. What are you doing and who's screaming?" Rebecca asked.

"Oh, that's just the TV."

"Well, I got good news."

"Well, tell me. Don't leave me in suspense."

"I'm pregnant."

7

"Well, congratulations."

"Just thought you'd like to know."

"I'm happy for you. Do you want to celebrate? I can take you out to dinner."

"Okay, that sounds good."

"Is 5:30 p.m. good?"

"I'll see ya then," she replied.

Hanging up the phone, he headed back to Paco who was screaming louder than before, while he was trying to break the chains holding him to the cherry picker.

"You ready to talk now?" Spencer asked.

"Yes, please, just stop!" he begged.

"Okay, who hired you to kill Jerome?"

"A guy named Rick. He hung out over there in Miami Gardens at a place called King of Diamonds."

"That's it?"

"That's all I know."

Spencer pulled out his Glock 17 and shot Paco right between his eyes.

Turning to the other three people in the warehouse, he told them to clean up the mess and to get rid of the body. He headed over to his new Camaro and took off to find Rick.

FOUR

Ending the phone call to her brother, Rebecca turned to Smooth and said, "Me and Spencer are going to celebrate. Do you want to come?" she asked.

"Nah, go ahead and enjoy yourself. I got some stuff to take care of."

"You sure, babe?"

"Yeah. Have fun!" he said, as he stood up and stretched. Once he was standing, he gave her a big hug and kiss.

"See ya later," he said, walking to the front door.

"Walk and feed Zorro before you leave."

"I will," she answered.

Once downstairs, he climbed into his truck, started it, and headed to Roxy's. Once there, he headed straight to his table. As soon as he sat down, the waitress showed up.

"What would you like to drink?" she asked.

"Give me a Coke, no ice."

"Alright. I'll be right back," she said, heading to get his drink.

Looking around the restaurant, Smooth saw Roxy talking to a few older women.

"Here's your drink. Do you want to order, or do you need more time?"

"Give me chicken strips and mozzarella cheese sticks."

"Alright, I'll be back with it!" she replied, as she walked to the back to give the cook his order. A few minutes later, Roxy came over and sat down.

"Hey, Smooth."

"Hey, Roxy."

"What ya up to?" she asked.

"Just figured I'd have lunch here before I start my day, plus I wanted to see how you're doing?"

"Busy! Other than that, I'm good. So, you going to see China this weekend?"

"Yeah, I'm going. What about you?" he asked.

"Not this week, but I will next week."

"Here's your food," the waitress said, as she set it down in front of Smooth.

"Anything else?" the waitress asked.

"Nah, I'm good. Thanks."

"Well, I'm going back to work. Enjoy your meal," Roxy said, as she headed off to talk to an older couple.

Smooth dug in, enjoying every bite. Suddenly, his phone started to ring.

"Hello?" he asked.

"Hey, it's me, Ronny. Where ya at?"

"I'm at Roxy's."

"I'll be there in 10 minutes. So please wait!" Ronny said, as he ended the call.

Hmmm . . . wonder what that's about? Smooth thought to himself, as he went back to enjoying his meal. About 15 minutes later, Ronny entered and she was led to Smooth's table by a waitress.

"I just need a Coke. I already ate," Ronny said, as he sat down at the table.

"So, what brings you around here? Better yet, just tell me what's going on," Smooth inquired.

"Well, our money has been coming up short at one certain spot. I looked into it and I think I found what the problem is."

"And what's that?"

"One of our people is using our product."

"Please tell me you're joking!"

"I wish I was, but I'm 100% sure about this."

"So, what do you think we should do?" Smooth asked.

"Not sure yet, but one of us will think of something."

* * *

Noticing that it was 5:45 p.m., Sue picked up his phone and called the girl from the car wash.

"Hello?" she answered.

"Waz up, ma?"

"Who's this?"

11

"Sue Rabbit."

"Who?"

"You gave me your number at the carwash."

"Oh yeah. So, what's up?" she asked.

"You ready for me to come pick you up?"

"Yeah, I'm ready. Pick me up at the Wal-Mart on 27th."

"I'll be there in five minutes."

"See ya then," she said, as she ended the call.

Five minutes later, he pulled up to the Wal-Mart. He couldn't help the smile on his face. She was standing there looking sexy as hell. He pulled up in front of her and rolled down the passenger side window.

"You ready?" he asked.

"Yep!" she said, as she got into his car and put on her seatbelt.

"Well, this is weird," he said.

"Why?"

"'Cause I don't even know your name," he replied.

"My name's Sharon, but everyone calls me Cherry."

"Well, my name's Trayvon Jackson, but everyone calls me Sue Rabbit. Sue for short."

"Well, Sue. Where are we going?" she asked.

"I told you I'd take you anywhere you wanted."

"Well, I'm not a high-class girl, so let's just go to Pizza Hut."

"Sounds good to me."

* * *

"Hello?" Smooth said, answering his phone.

"Hey mon, can I talk wit Smooth?"

"It's me, Stone. Waz up?"

"I need tin of those tings."

"When do you need them?"

"Today or tomorrow," Stone replied.

"Alright, meet me at the gas station in one hour."

"See yous der!"

Smooth turned on his radio, blasting Drake's new song as he headed home. Arriving at home, he opened his door and he was almost knocked down as Zorro jumped all over him.

After petting Zorro, Smooth grabbed the dog's leash.

"You ready for a walk, boy?" Smooth said, while attaching the leash. As the elevator door opened, Smooth noticed an older white couple looking nervous. He wasn't sure if it was because he was black or because of Zorro.

"Hello," Smooth said when he stepped onto the elevator. The man returned the greeting to Smooth.

They all exited the elevator on the bottom floor. The older couple headed for the garage while Zorro led Smooth in another direction. As he turned the corner, Smooth saw two beautiful women walking a German Shepherd. Both dogs began to smell each other in a dog-greeting manner.

"Hey, nice dog!" the one holding the leash said.

"Yeah, but he's a handful sometimes!"

"Can I pet him?" the other girl asked.

"Sure, if ya want to lose an arm!" Smooth replied.

"What?"

"Just joking. He don't bite," Smooth laughed.

The girl bent down and started to pet Zorro.

"So, do you live around here?" asked the one holding the leash.

"Yeah, I do. I live in the next building."

"I live in this building."

"Well, my name is Smooth . . . and that's Zorro."

"My name is Jessica . . . and that's Nina."

"Nice to meet you. Do you always walk this way?"

"I walk wherever Nina takes me," Jessica said.

"Same with me. Well, I hope to see you again."

"Yeah. I hope so, too."

"Come on, Zorro. Time to go, buddy," Smooth said, as they headed back to the apartment.

FIVE

Opening her eyes, the white light was blinding. She was confused and unsure of where she was, as she tried to sit up and open her eyes.

"Hey there. Glad to see you're awake," a strange voice said.

"Where am I? What happened?"

Finally, her eyes adjusted to the light, and she looked around. It looked like she was in a hospital.

"I remember fighting a girl and that's it."

"Well, you were stabbed three times. Lucky you recovered. The doctors were really worried when you first got here."

"What day is it? How long have I been here?" China asked.

"It's Thursday. You've been here since Monday."

"Has my family been informed?"

"Nah. We only do that if you die. Honestly, I don't know. Why? Are you expecting a visit?" the officer asked.

"Yeah. I'm expecting my fiancé, my mother, and my sister."

"I'm not sure what will happen, but I will look into it for you, okay?"

"Thank you. When's chow? I'm starving."

"Just grab that remote and push the button that says nurse. And when she comes, tell her you're hungry."

China pushed the red button. The nurse popped up a few seconds later.

"Well, well. Look who woke up. What can I get you?" the nurse asked.

"I'm starving! Anyway, I can get something to eat?"

"Sure, what you want?"

"Anything!"

Okay, I'll be back in a few."

When the nurse returned, she had a tray full of food.

"Not sure what you'd like, so I grabbed a little of everything: hamburger, chicken sandwich, Doritos, Fritos, crackers, cookies. Hopefully, you will eat something. You need to eat to get your strength back."

"Thank you. Don't worry, I'm gonna eat. I'm so hungry, I might eat it all," China laughed.

"Enjoy. Just push the button if you need anything else," the nurse said, as she headed out the door.

After finishing her meal, she asked if she could use the phone.

"Sorry, but it's against the rules. It's considered a security risk. Wish I could give you one."

"Damn, so how long will I be here?"

"That's up to the doctors. It shouldn't take that long. He should be by soon, and we will ask him. In the meantime, why don't you sit back and enjoy something on cable TV," the guard responded.

Flipping through all the channels, she saw lots of stuff that looked interesting. Finally, she chose a movie where Jennifer Lopez dated a rich white man. It was funny, too. Halfway through the movie, China got thirsty, so she pushed the nurse button.

"What ya need?" the nurse asked, when she walked in the door.

"I'm thirsty. Can I get something to drink?"

"Sure. What do you want?"

"Anything, as long as it's wet," China joked.

When the nurse returned, she set down a tray in front of China.

"Well, we have Pepsi, Coke, Sierra Mist, Fruit Punch, milk, and strawberry milk. So what will it be?"

"I'll take the Pepsi."

SIX

Arriving at the Pizza Hut, Sue ran around to the passenger side to open Cherry's door. But, before he got halfway there, she opened her door and got out.

"Damn, Cherry. Can't you wait for a brother to open the door?"

"Why would I? My hands and feet work just fine. But I appreciate the thought."

Walking to the front door, Sue grabbed the door and opened it.

"Ladies first!" he said.

"Ahhh, the perfect gentleman."

"Yes, that's me!"

Picking a table in the back and sitting down, Sue's eyes wandered around as he checked out his surroundings.

"So, what you gonna get?" she asked.

"Deep dish . . . meat lovers," he replied.

"Well, I'll have the same."

When the waitress came over, Sue ordered for the both of them.

"So, you come to Pizza Hut a lot?" he asked.

"Every now and then. What about you?"

"Ummm . . . not much. I prefer Denny's or Ryan's Steakhouse."

"I like Taco Bell, Burger King, and Pizza Hut. Not really into any fancy places like Olive Garden, Red Lobster, or shit like that!"

"Well, that's good to know."

"Why's it good to know?

"Ya know, for future reference."

"So, you plan on more than one date?"

"Well, yeah. What, you thought this was a one-time booty call or something?" he asked.

"Well, that's what usually happens. Once I sleep with them, they disappear."

"I'm not like that!"

"You don't have a problem with my age?"

"You're 17, right? How long 'til you're 18?"

"Yeah, I'm 17, but will be 18 in a few months."

"How many months?"

"Two and a half."

"Here's your pizza," the waitress said, setting down the pizza. "Be careful, it's hot," she warned them, as she walked away

* * *

Seeing Stone leaning up against the car, Smooth looked around to see if anything was out of place. Not noticing anything out of the ordinary, he pulled into the parking lot and pulled up to Stone's car. Smooth got out and walked around to the trunk. He

19

popped the trunk with his key fob, and then reached in and grabbed a bag.

"Hey mon!"

"Hey Stone. Waz up?"

"Notin' mon. You got dos tin thins?"

"Yep, right here!" Smooth replied, handing Stone the bag. Stone popped his trunk and threw the bag in, and then pulled out another one and handed it to Smooth.

"Here, mon. Tanks! See ya nex' time!"

"Just call me, Stone," Smooth said, closing his trunk and walking around to the driver's seat.

Smooth got into his car and headed back to his place to drop off the money. He then decided to go to Ronny's to pick up the money there as well. Pulling up to Ronny's, he saw his white Lexus RX 350 Sport. He got out of his car, looked around, and saw nothing out of place. After knocking on the door, Smooth waited for Ronny to answer. After a few more knocks, Ronny answered the door in boxers and a towel hanging off his shoulder.

"What's up?"

"Just figured I'd stop by to see what's up and to see if you came up with how to handle that problem."

"Well, I was in the shower. Let me dry off and get dressed, and we will talk," Ronny said, walking off down the hallway. "Help yourself to the bar," he called out back over his shoulder.

Smooth went over to the counter, poured himself a glass of rum, and said, "Mmmm . . . this tastes good."

Ronny walked in a few minutes later.

"Well, have you come up with a plan?" Smooth asked.

"Hmm . . . we have two choices. Kill him and be done with it or bring him over here and try to scare him straight, while letting him know we're here to help."

"So, which one's best?"

"Well, a few sayings come to mind. Those who seek to achieve things should show no mercy. And to have ultimate victory, you must be ruthless. So I'd say it's best to kill him and make an example out of him," Ronny said.

"Well, I'd say we do it and make an example. Call everyone over here for a meeting in one hour."

"Will do. Be right back," Ronny said. He then left and walked back in with his cell phone to his ear. He then spent the next 10 minutes calling everyone.

"Okay, it's done! Everyone will be here within the next hour," Ronny said.

While waiting for everyone to show up, Smooth's mind turned to Rebecca and China, and in what manner China was going to react. He hated the fact that he couldn't tell her privately, but had to do it in front of a bunch of other inmates and their visitors.

* * *

Climbing out of the bathtub, Rebecca started to dry off. She saw her reflection in the floor-to-ceiling mirror. She pushed out her belly trying to see how she'd look when she started showing. She was super-excited to be a mom since she always wanted kids.

There was only one problem: China. How would her kid have two moms? Rebecca was straight with herself, China, and Smooth. But now that she was pregnant, she was not sure about the threesome. So how could she get Smooth all to herself? China had some time before she would get out, so Rebecca still had time to come up with a plan.

It was time for her to get dressed. She wanted to look nice for her brother's congratulations party. Rebecca picked out a low-slung black Givenchy dress with a pair of three-inch heels. Looking in the mirror, she thought, I'm sexy! Splashing on some Rogue by Rihanna, she left the bathroom, as Zorro jumped up and almost knocked her over.

"Damn it, Zorro! Get down! Can't you see I'm dressed up? I don't need dog hair all over me," she told him. Rebecca then went to the kitchen to feed the dog, just as her phone rang.

"Hello?" she answered.

"Hey sis, it's me. Are you ready?" Spencer asked.

"Yeah, I'm ready."

"I'm on my way up," he said, disconnecting the call.

Five minutes later, there was a knock on the door. Zorro started barking and ran for the door.

"Get back, Zorro!" Rebecca yelled, as she unlocked the door. The dog tried to run out; however, Rebecca grabbed his collar and pulled him back in.

"Easy there, fella," Spencer said.

Rebecca came out and closed the door behind her.

"That dog is just too much sometimes. But I love him."

"Well sis, you look nice tonight."

"Thank you," Spencer responded, as they got on the elevator. Pushing the button for the bottom floor, Spencer straightened his tie.

"Well, that was nice of you to dress all fancy, but we are only going to McDonald's," he joked.

"Hey, look at you. I'm not the only one who dressed, up."

SEVEN

With everyone gathered around him, Smooth got everyone quiet.

"Alright, everyone. The reason we are all here is simple. Someone is messing with my money by using our product. I treat y'all real good, and pay you all good. All I ask is respect and loyalty. Now, Freddy, come here."

"What's up, boss?" Freddy asked.

Smooth pulled out his FN Five Seven, put it to Freddy's head, and pulled the trigger, blowing Freddy's brains all over the place.

"Respect and loyalty. That's all I ask. If you need money or you have a problem, call me, okay?"

They all nodded their heads in agreement.

"I hated doing what I just did, but I won't be disrespected. Now, clean up this mess up and get rid of the body."

"I will do it myself," Prince Guru said.

"You know how?" Smooth asked.

"Well, let's just say it's not my first time disposing of a dead body!"

"Alright then . . . now that that's taken care of, everyone get back to work."

Turning to Ronny, Smooth asked, "Do you think that worked? Or do you think we will have more problems?"

"I think you got the point across. They'd be suicidal if they tried anything now."

"How are you on the product?" Smooth asked.

"We are pretty low," Ronny responded.

"Okay, I'll get some more to you by tomorrow. I gotta go and re-up this weekend while I visit China. So, I will give you enough to get by until I get back."

"Sounds good to me," Ronny said, as he pulled a black backpack out from behind the couch.

"Here's your money from the last trip," Ronny said.

"Alright. I'm gonna get ghost and take care of business."

"See ya tomorrow," Ronny said to Smooth, as Smooth walked out the door.

Ten minutes later, Smooth was knocking on Amanda's apartment door.

"Hey sexy!" Smooth said to Amanda, as she opened the door.

"Hey yourself. Come on in."

Smooth followed her to the kitchen.

"I need you to cook some of those things for me."

"Okay, want something to drink?"

"No, but I want something to eat!" he replied.

"What you want to eat?"

"You!" he said, as he pulled her to himself. Kissing her deeply, Smooth started to pull her shirt off. He then got on his knees and began to roll her pants down. She wasn't wearing any panties.

"Lean over the table!" Smooth told her, and then he smacked her ass. Once she turned around and bent over the table, he scooted over and started to eat her pussy nice and slow. He slid his tongue in and out of her tight pussy.

"Oh God! I'm gonna cummm!" she panted.

When he heard that, he stopped.

"What the fuck! Why'd you stop?"

"Shut up and stay bent over!"

When she bent back over the table, Smooth went back to eating out her pussy. But when he heard her breathing hard, he started to suck on her clit while sliding two fingers in her soaking-wet pussy.

"Here I cummmmm . . . ! Goddamn! I'm cumminnnggg!"

After she recovered, Smooth stood up and slid his dick right into her tight pussy, going deep but soft.

"Fuck me hard!" she ordered.

Smooth grabbed her hips and began to fuck her hard and fast.

"Oh, yeah. Fuck me, daddy!" she screamed.

Going all the way in hard and fast, Smooth then slid out until he got put the tip in her. He then slammed back in hard and fast. Her moans and screams were really turning him on. Not being able to hold back any longer, he shot his hot cum all up in her pussy, causing her to cum again.

"Hang on a second!" Amanda said, as she grabbed a towel and wet it. She walked over to him and cleaned the cum and pussy juice off his cock.

"Thanks," he said.

"Let me go clean up, and then I'll be right back."

A few minutes later, Amanda returned to the kitchen wearing a pink Juicy Couture sweat suit.

"So, how many ya got for me?" she asked.

"Got five and your money's in the bag with the work."

"It will take me a few days, ya know."

"Can you at least have three for me tomorrow?"

"Yeah. No problem!"

"Well, I need to get on home. See ya tomorrow."

* * *

Walking into the restaurant, Spencer and Rebecca were greeted by a hostess.

"Table for two, please," Spencer said.

"Right this way."

Walking to the table, Rebecca looked around. It looked like a very old house lit with candles. It was a very romantic place.

"Here is your table."

A waitress soon appeared and asked, "What would you like to drink?"

"Give us a bottle of wine," Spencer said.

"Alright. I'll be right back," she said, as she walked away.

Looking at the menu, Rebecca noticed that the prices were sky high.

"Everything is too expensive!"

'Don't worry about it. We're celebrating, right? So let's enjoy it."

"Alright. If you're paying!" she said.

"Yeah, I'm paying, so order away."

When the waitress came back with a bottle of wine and two glasses, she asked if they were ready to order.

27

"Yes. I'll have the thick-cut prime rib with a baked potato and salad," Rebecca ordered.

"I'll have the battered pork chops with mashed potatoes and some dinner rolls," Spencer ordered.

"Can't believe my little sister gonna be a mom."

"Well, believe it!"

"So, is it Smooth's?" Spencer inquired.

"Yes, it's his. He's the only one I've been with since I've been out of prison."

"Does he treat you good?"

"He treats me like a queen. I've never had anyone show me as much love as he has," she said truthfully.

"All that matters is that he treats you good. As long as you're happy, it's all good."

"Here's your food," the waitress said, as she set it down on the table.

"Let me know if you all need anything else."

"We will," Spencer replied.

Grabbing the wine, Spencer poured two glasses and set one in front of Rebecca.

"I don't think I should have alcohol now that I'm pregnant."

"Don't worry! A few glasses of wine ain't gonna kill ya."

"Alright," she said, as she grabbed her glass.

Raising his glass for a toast, Spencer said, "To a bright future!"

"To a bright future."

* * *

"So, do you plan on going to college after high school?" Sue asked Cherry before taking a big bite of his pizza.

"I'd like to go to college," she replied, as she wiped her mouth with a napkin. She then took another bite.

"What do you want to major in?"

"I'd like to be a veterinarian."

"So, you like animals?"

"I love animals!"

"I thought about getting a dog."

"What kind?"

"I like German Shepherds. Pit bulls and Rottweilers are overrated."

"I have a chocolate lab and I love him to death," she gushed.

"Labs are good, too."

"So, are you going to college or have you been?" she asked.

"Nope. No college for me."

"Why not?" she asked.

"Let's just say they don't have classes to learn the things I do for a living."

"And what do you do for a living?"

"That's a secret. If I told ya, I'd have to kill ya," he joked.

"I like that. A man of mystery. That's sexy. Like hooking up with James Bond."

"So, you like that?"

"Hell yeah! The mystery and bad boy act is a total turn-on."

"Well, I'm a mysterious bad boy. Does that turn you on?"

Instead of answering him, she put her foot between his legs and started to rub his dick.

"So, what do you think?" she asked.

"Got one question."

"What's that?"

"Your place or mine?" he asked.

"Yours."

After waving to the waitress, he paid the bill, tipped the waitress, and then both nearly ran to the car. Back at his place, they both stripped naked and she stopped and looked at his erect dick.

"O.M.G.! I don't think I can take all that!" She got down on her knees and started stroking his hard dick, while she looked up at him. After a minute of stroking, she put it in her mouth. Only being able to put half in her mouth, she used her hands to massage his nuts and stroke him.

"Wait, Cherry!"

"Wait! Why?" she asked.

"'Cause I don't want to cum so soon!" he said, as he led her to the couch, laid her down, and started to kiss her from her pussy, taking care to massage her clit while tongue-fucking her.

"Oh, yes! Right there!" she moaned.

A few minutes later, her breathing came in gasps and her pussy began to spasm. After licking all her cum up, he stood up, pulled her toward the end of the couch, put her feet on his shoulders, and slid inside her dripping pussy.

"Oh . . . wait! Go slow!" she begged.

He slowly but surely got his whole cock inside her. Once she was used to the feeling, he began to pick up speed. After a few minutes, he stopped and pulled out.

"Get on your hands and knees!" he demanded.

Once on her knees, he put his dick back into her pussy and fucked her hard, until he busted a nut deep inside her.

"Damn, I really needed that!" she said.

"So, do you have a curfew, or can you stay the night?"

"I'll stay. Let me call my sister to let her know I'm staying with a friend."

Without even getting dressed, she grabbed her phone and started dialing. Then Sue heard a one-sided conversation.

"Hey sis. Look, I'm staying with Shelly tonight, so don't wait up for me ... Yep ... Uh huh ... Sure ... I will ... I love you, too ... Alright, bye."

"Okay, that's done. Now what are you planning?" she asked.

"Figured we'd just lie around and watch movies."

"Sounds good. Now let's pick a movie.

EIGHT

China woke up and felt a sharp pain in her side. She felt confused and had a moment of panic, until she remembered she was at the hospital. She figured she fell asleep watching TV. Looking around the room, she saw two guards watch the television.

"Has the doctor come by yet?" she asked.

"Yeah," one officer said. "You'll probably be out of here on Monday."

"I need to let my family know not to drive up here this weekend. They are probably worried since I haven't called."

"Well, there is nothing we can do about it," the heavy officer said.

"Can you at least call them and let them know not to come?"

"No can do!" he said as he stood up.

"I'm going to grab some coffee and use the restroom. You want anything?" the officer asked.

"Yeah, I'll take some coffee since you're getting some."

"Cream or sugar?"

"Both please."

"Alright."

"Look, I could get fired for this but, I want to help you," the other officer said, as he pulled out his cell phone.

"What's the phone number and name?" he asked.

"555-6108 . . . and the name is Smooth."

"Okay," the guard replied, as he dialed the number.

China listened to the one-sided conversation.

"Yes, can I talk to Smooth? Hey, Smooth. I'm calling for China. . . . No, she's okay, just had a little accident. Look, I'm not supposed to do this, but I'm trying to help y'all. . . . Yes! Yes! . . . Well, she won't be allowed to have visits this week, so you'll have to visit next weekend . . . "Yes, I'll tell her. Alright, bye!"

Ending the call, the guard turned to China and said, "He said he loves you and can't wait to see you."

"Thank you so much," she said.

"Make sure this stays between us. Because I could lose my job for that."

"Don't worry. I won't tell a soul. I owe you one. Not sure how I'll pay you, but I owe you."

* * *

Getting to his apartment parking lot, Smooth ended the call. He was worried to death over China and he was unsure who the man was. He wondered if

33

Roxy had heard from her. So Smooth pulled back out and headed to Roxy's. After arriving at the restaurant, Smooth asked the waitress to tell Roxy that he was there. He then headed to his table and waited for her. The waitress returned with a drink.

"Coke, no ice, right?" she asked.

"Yeah!"

"Roxy said she'll be over in a few minutes. Do you want to order?"

"I'll take the fried chicken, corn, and dinner rolls."

"Coming right up," the waitress said.

Five minutes later, Roxy came over.

"What's up, Smooth?"

"Have you heard from China lately?"

"Not for a few days. Why?"

"I just got a call from a dude saying she had an accident and won't be able to have visitors this weekend. So I'm worried."

"What kinda accident?"

"Not sure, which is why I'm worried."

"Did you call the prison?"

"No, because the dude said he'd get fired if they found out he called me."

"Well, I say let's wait until Tuesday. If we haven't heard something by them, we'll call. Okay?"

"Okay."

"Try not to worry so much. She probably sprained an ankle or something playing volleyball."

"Yeah, you're right!" he confessed.

"Here's your food," the waitress said, as she set the plate down in front of him.

"Well, I guess I need to get back to work. Hope you enjoy your meal."

"I will. I always enjoy the food here!" he said.

"Let me know if you need anything."

Smooth then began to eat.

* * *

"So, how'd ya meet Smooth?" Spencer asked.

"Well, while I was in prison, I had a roommate named China. Smooth is her fiancé. She said I could stay in their guest room. But now it's awkward."

"What do you mean awkward?"

"Well, you know I'm bisexual."

"Yeah!"

"Well, me and China were lovers. She wanted a three-way relationship with me, her, and Smooth. So I got out and began sleeping with Smooth. And now I'm pregnant and have no clue how China's gonna take this."

"Yeah, that is awkward. So, what do you plan on doing?"

"Smooth is gonna tell her in person during visit. Guess I will wait and see how she reacts before I make any decisions."

"Sounds like a good idea. But be prepared for the worst," he warned her.

"You know, at first I thought the threesome would be awesome. I truly love China. But now that I'm out and met Smooth, I truly love him. They are the two loves of my life, so this arrangement was awesome. But now that I'm pregnant, I'm having second thoughts. How can I let my child grow up with one dad, but two mothers?"

"Yeah, I can understand all that. I honestly don't know what to tell you. I've never run into anything like this. Best I can tell you is to follow your heart."

"That's the problem. I love them both!" she exclaimed.

"But who do you love the most?" he asked.

"I honestly don't know. I love them both."

"Well, what do you think is best for the baby? You got to think what's best for the baby. It's not just you now."

"I know. God, what am I gonna do?"

"Hey, let's calm down. Let's change the subject to something else. We are supposed to be celebrating. Right?"

"Yeah, you're right!"

"When are you gonna pick a name?" he asked.

"Well, I got to find out if it's a boy or girl."

"Oh yeah. Guess that would be a good idea. Sorry, I'm not good at this. Never been around a pregnant woman."

"Hell, I've never been pregnant, so this is new to both of us!"

"Cheers to you and other mothers!" Spencer said, as he raised his glass toward Rebecca. She raised hers as well.

"Cheers!" she said. She then took a drink of her wine.

"So, now that you're out of the army, what do you do?" she asked.

"Let's just say that I take care of other people's problems."

"Like what?"

"Sis, it's best that you don't know. Sorry, but it's for your own good."

"Hmmm . . . So, you're a super-secret agent?" she laughed.

"Very funny!"

"So what are your plans?" he asked.

"Well, I've been taking classes online."

"What type of classes?"

"College classes to be a nurse."

"Are you gonna keep taking them?"

"Yeah. It's something I really want. Plus, it will help me have my own money and help me take care of my baby."

"So, you want your independence?"

"Yeah!"

"And I wanna do it legally. I want to actually work for a living."

"That's funny."

"Why?" he asked.

"Because there are millions of Americans that bust their asses every day wishing that they didn't have to work."

"I'd trade them. Now that I think about it, it is funny," she laughed.

NINE

Banga had two drinks to celebrate. He just left the courthouse where he found out that the charges against him were dropped. He was so happy. He could finally go back to Miami. But he wasn't sure what he wanted to do because he had begun to like this place. First, he'd go celebrate at the Cotton Club with Meka and Ham in tow.

"So, now that you're free, what are you gonna do?" Meka asked.

"Honestly, I don't know. At first, I hated this place, but I've come to love it. And it's good money," Banga said.

"Well, we would love to have you stay," Ham replied.

"Nigga, you just want the money," Banga said.

"Hey, that might be true, but I got mad love for ya," Ham said.

"What about you, Meka?" Banga asked.

"I like having you around," she replied.

"Well, time to get back to work," Banga said.

Pulling his cell phone out of his pocket, he dialed Smooth's number.

"Yeah?" Smooth asked.

"It's me, Banga!"

"Wuz up, B?" Smooth asked.

"Well, I got good news. They dropped all the charges against me."

"That's great! So when ya coming home?"

"I'm not sure. I kinda like this place and its good money. Don't get me wrong, I love y'all and miss ya, but I don't know. My mind says go home, but my head says stay here."

"So, you gonna still hustle?"

"Hell yeah! As a matter of fact, I need to re-up."

"I'll bring you a few keys tomorrow."

"Meka will be excited to hear that you're coming."

"I bet she will. Well, let me get off here and get back to work."

"See ya, tomorrow," Smooth told him. Ending the call, Banga slid the phone back into his pocket and headed over to Meka.

"Your boyfriend will be coming back tomorrow."

"You know I don't have a boyfriend," Meka said.

"I'm talking about Smooth."

"Oh my God! Are you kidding?" she asked excitedly.

"Nope. I'm serious. Now I need to go find Ham," Banga said, as he walked away. Finding him, Banga pulled him away from some hot chick.

"What the hell?" Ham asked. "I was trying to get that number."

"Smooth will be here tomorrow. So, I'll need you to do your magic."

"No problem. Now, shouldn't you be celebrating?"

"Yeah, guess I should. Later!"

Walking to the bar, Banga started watching the dance floor, hoping to spot a date for the night. His phone started to vibrate. Banga went to the bathroom for a little privacy.

"Hello?" he asked. Then he heard an automated voice.

This is a collect call from Jacob Spears, an inmate at Martin County Jail. If you want to accept the call, press zero.

Banga pressed zero.

This call may be recorded and monitored. Thank you for using G.T.L.

"Hello!"

"Hey Kentucky! What's good?"

"Well, I finally got my first book published, thanks to a dude Ray Brown. I didn't have anyone to tell or celebrate with, so I called you."

"Well, congratulations!"

"Thanks. I also wanted to thank you for the money you sent."

"No problem. Just let me know when you need more."

"I will. So, what are they gonna do with you?"

"They dropped all my charges, so I'm free!"

"Damn! We both got something to celebrate," Kentucky said.

"Yeah, and the weird part is that today is Friday the 13th."

"Oh shit. You're right!"

You have one minute left, said the automated voice.

"Well, take care and feel free to call me whenever."

"Alright!"

Thank you for using G.T.L., the automated voice said before it disconnected.

Banga put his phone away and then headed back to the bar to find a date. After he sat down, he noticed a light-skinned redbone in a tight, black mini skirt and tight spaghetti-strap shirt. Catching her attention, he waved to her to join him. She walked over.

"Can I buy you a drink?" Banga asked.

"Yeah, a White Russian."

"What's that?"

"It's Kahlua and vodka."

"Bartender, can I get two White Russians."

Turning back to her, Banga saw not only her thick ass, but also a beautiful woman.

"My name is Banga."

"My name is Sonja," she answered, putting out her hand.

Shaking her hand was somewhat exotic, because when she shook his hand, her breasts jiggled.

"Not trying to be the Average Joe, but do you come here often?" he asked.

"Every Friday and Saturday. What about you?"

"Nah, this is only my second time in here."

"Need another drink?"

"Yeah," she replied, as she downed the rest of hers.

"Here ya go!" the bartender said.

"Thanks," Banga said, as he handed the drink to Sonja.

"So, what do you do for a living, Banga?" she asked.

"Well, I'd say retail."

"Funny."

TEN

Smooth loading his bag and put four kilos inside it. He figured Banga would want that instead of his usual two. Smooth then dialed a number and headed to the kitchen.

"Hello?" someone answered.

"Yes, can I talk to Jefe?"

"May I ask who you are?"

"Please tell Jefe it's Smooth."

After a few minutes, Jefe came on the line.

"Smooth. How are you, my friend?"

"I'm good. What are you up to?"

"Not much. How can I help you?"

"I need 30 of those."

"When do you plan to be here?" Jefe asked.

"Between lunch and dinner."

"Sounds good. See ya then."

Ending the call, Smooth grabbed Zorro's leash.

"Yeah, buddy. Time for a walk!" Smooth said, as the dog got all excited and bounced up and down. Finally getting the leash on the dog, Smooth headed out the door. Once outside, Zorro took off to the left where he met the women the day before. Unfortunately, he didn't see them. So as soon as Zorro was done, Smooth took the dog back inside the apartment. Smooth then took off the leash and grabbed his phone to call Rebecca.

"Hello?" she answered.

"Hey it's me. Look, I'm gonna be gone for a few days, so I need you to feed, water, and walk Zorro."

"Okay, no problem. When are you leaving?"

"In a few minutes."

"Okay, see you when ya get back."

"Yeah!"

"And drive careful and stay safe," she added.

With everything taken care of, Smooth grabbed his bag and headed off to the garage. Throwing the bag into the back seat of his Ram, he got in and took off.

After arriving in Stuart, he headed to Banga's house. Once there, he got out, grabbed the backpack, and looked around. Seeing no one, he went to the door and waited. Finally, Meka answered the door, with a blunt in her mouth.

"Hey sexy! What's up? Come on in!" she said, as she leaned back holding the door open for him. Once inside, he saw Banga and Ham on the couch placing a video game. Pizza boxes were over all over the table. Hearing someone come in, Banga saw that it was Smooth, so he paused the game.

"What the fuck!" Ham yelled, until he saw Smooth.

"What's up?" Banga asked.

"Nothing. Got you four of those things," Smooth said, as he tossed the bag to Banga.

Banga got up and walked to the closet. He reached in and pulled out another backpack.

"Here's the money for the last stuff," Banga said, handing over the bag to Smooth.

Looking over at Meka, Smooth said, "Let me put this in my truck, and I'll be right back."

"I'll be waiting."

After running to the truck, he returned but didn't see Meka anywhere.

"In the bedroom," Banga said.

Smooth walked into the bedroom and saw Meka butt naked and spread out on the bed. Smooth stripped naked and walked over to the bed. He began to stroke his cock. When he got on the bed, Meka stopped him.

"Waz wrong?"

'Lay down. I want to be in charge this time."

Smooth lay on his back and watched as Meka took his cock in her mouth and sucked.

"Mmm . . . mmm," she moaned, taking each inch and deep throating him. As he fixed to cum, she stopped. She then moved up, straddled him, and slowly slid down onto his hard cock.

"Damn! I can feel you deep inside me," she moaned. As she rode up and down on his cock, Smooth watched as it disappeared in and out. Then he used one hand to play with her clit as she took his dick.

Playing with her clit caused her to cum fast, as she screamed, "Oh my God!"

"Ummm . . . sorry!" she said, as she continued to ride him.

He watched her ride him and make sexy faces, which made him cum deep inside her pussy.

"Damn, that was good!" Meka said,

"Sure was!"

Meka started to put on her clothes and then Smooth got up and did the same.

"So, when will I see ya next?" she asked.

"I'll be back in a few days. I gotta go to New York and I'll stop by on my way back."

"I will be waiting."

* * *

Done with their dinner, Spencer asked Rebecca, "Are you ready for dessert?"

"Hell yeah!"

Flagging down the waitress, Spencer ordered them both German chocolate cake.

"I can already taste it."

"Guess having a baby increases your appetite."

47

"I did eat a lot, huh?" she laughed.

"Here's your cake," the waitress said. "So, what's the special occasion?"

"I'm having a baby."

"Congratulations. You make a great couple."

"Oh no! He's my brother!" they all laughed.

"Let me know if you need anything else," the waitress informed.

"Mmmmm . . . German chocolate cake and wine make a great combination," Rebecca said.

"Yes they do. So eat and drink all you can. Remember, this is a special occasion."

"Don't worry. I'm going to eat and drink until I can't eat and drink anymore."

A few minutes later, Spencer sat back and announced, "I'm stuffed!"

"Yeah, me, too, and I got a buzz," she laughed.

Flagging down the waitress, he asked for the check. When she returned with it, Spencer showed it to Rebecca.

"She actually gave you her number!"

"Yeah. Seems to happen a lot."

"Do you ever call them?"

"Yeah, I do call back some of them. But some I just throw away. Like this waitress, I'm gonna call her back."

"Why call her back?" Rebecca asked.

"Because, one . . . she's hot! And she don't seem to be crazy. You'd be so surprised at some of the crazy women I've picked up."

"She is kinda hot. I can see that. And if she gave me her number, I'd call back, too. So, what are we doing now?"

"Figured we'd watch a movie."

"Oh, I want to see the new Batman vs. Superman."

"Well, that's what we'll watch."

* * *

"Damn, ma!"

"Thought this would wake you up," Cherry said.

"Oh, believe me. I'm awake!"

"Good!" Cherry said, as she went back to sucking his cock. Deep throating him and humming, the vibrations had him ready to cum.

"If you don't stop, I'm gonna cum!"

"Hmmmm . . . hmmm!" she increased the speed until he shot his load down her throat, making sure she got the last drop.

"My turn!" he said.

"Nope, I don't have time. I got to get to school."

"Shit! I forgot you still go to school."

"Well, get up and get dressed before I'm late."

"Late?"

"Yeah, genius! You gotta drive me."

"Okay, give me five minutes."

Sue hopped in the shower, cleaned up quickly, and got dressed. They he headed out.

"I'm ready," he yelled.

After getting in the car, he asked if she had time to go out for breakfast.

"No, but we can go to the drive-through."

"Bet!" he said, as he pulled into the McDonald's

"Can I help, you?" the voice asked from the speaker.

"Yeah, let me get four sausage, egg, and cheese biscuits with two hash browns."

After getting their food, she opened one bags, grabbed a hash brown, and put it in the biscuit.

"So, honestly. Is this a one-night thing or am I gonna see you again?"

"Oh, you'll definitely see more of me. At least until you don't want to see me anymore."

"Good. Call me tonight," she said, as they pulled into the school parking lot. Then she leaned over to kiss him before getting out of the car.

"I'll call tonight," he said.

"You better!" she replied.

ELEVEN

"So, what do you two want to watch?" China asked.

"It don't matter. You pick. I'm gonna watch my own movie on my phone," one of the guards replied.

"I could care less," the heavy guard said.

China picked a move called Jumpers, which she thought was very good. After it was over, she watched Limitless, which she also thought was another good movie. Then she lowered her bed and lay there thinking about shit.

Can't believe I got stabbed for nothing. Huh, I wonder how Rebecca and Smooth are doing, she thought. Two people she loved and missed dearly. She couldn't wait to be home with both of them. She then felt nasty since she was unable to shower.

"Everything all right?" a nurse walked in and asked.

"Yeah, but can I take a shower?"

"No, but I can give you a sponge bath."

"Well, can I at least get some privacy?"

"Can you two step outside, while I give her a bath?" the nurse asked.

"Yeah," the one cop replied, as they both left the room.

"We will be right out here," the fat guard reminded them.

Once they stepped out of the room, the nurse got some hot water from the sink and helped China sponge herself clean.

"So, if you don't mind me asking, what are you in prison for?"

"I got pulled over with a lot of drugs in my car."

"How much time do you got?"

"Well, I got sentenced to three years, but I only got about two left."

The nurse poured a special shampoo into China's hair and scrubbed it in.

"It's waterless shampoo," the nurse said.

"I didn't know they made that."

"Well, now that you're properly washed, what can I help you with?"

"I could use a grilled cheese sandwich and potato chips."

"One grilled cheese coming right up!" the nurse said, as she exited the room.

"Feel better?" the guard asked.

"A lot better. Thanks!"

"No problem."

The heavy guard sat back down and returned to his phone without saying a word. China went back to watching the movie.

"Here's your food."

"Thanks," China said, not realizing how hungry she was until she smelled the grilled cheese.

* * *

After eating, Spencer drove Rebecca back to her apartment. Once they parked, he went around and opened up her door. Spencer escorted her to her apartment to make sure that she got there safely. After making sure she was safe, he give her a hug and left. As soon as she closed the door, she locked it behind her. She then turned to Zorro who was going wild trying to get her attention. Damn, I shouldn't have drunk so much, she told herself. Gotta piss! She went to the bathroom. After relieving herself, she went back to the kitchen. She figured Zorro probably had to go outside as well, so she grabbed his leash.

"Come on, boy! Time for a walk!"

Zorro jumped all over the place.

"Stay still, boy, so I can get this damn leash on."

After finally getting the leash on the dog, they went downstairs. Once outside, she let Zorro take the lead. He went to the right and then stopped and smelled everything.

"Damn, I really should not have drunk so much," she again said to herself.

Her cell phone went off as she turned the corner.

53

"Hello?" she answered.

"Hey, babe!" Smooth said.

"How's your trip going?"

"Long and boring. You done celebrating?"

"Yes. Spencer and I went out for dinner, and then we went to see a movie. Spider Man vs. Batman . . . or maybe it was Batman vs. Spider Man."

"Are you okay?" he asked.

"Yeah, just drank too much wine."

"Where are you now? You're not driving, are you?"

"Nah, I'm walking Zorro. When I'm done, I'm gonna take a quick shower and then go to bed."

"Wish I was there to give you a bath."

"Me, too. But you'll be home soon enough."

"Yeah, but not soon enough!"

"Are you gonna go see China tomorrow?"

"No. Apparently, she had some kinda accident and can't have visits this weekend. But I'll see her next week."

"Alright. I'll talk to you later. If you need to talk or stay away, call me," she said.

"Okay. Later, babe!"

Ending the call, she looked around. Nobody was out at this time of night.

"Come on, Zorro! Time to head home!"

* * *

Sitting at the table in Ham's apartment, Banga was weighing the crack and packing it up in little bombs.

"Well, we should be good for a week," Banga said.

"Yeah," Ham agreed, bringing the last of the dope to the table to help Banga bag it all up.

"We need to get us another runner so we can have some on the back corner. 'Cause we gonna lose money if we don't."

"Okay! But until we find someone, I will set up shop on the back corner," Ham said.

"You sure you want to do that?" Banga asked.

"Someone's gotta do it, right?"

"We'll find a runner as soon as possible."

As soon as they bagged up the last of the dope and put it in bags, the door opened. Banga pulled out his .357, but it was only Meka.

"Damn, girl. You trying to get killed coming in the door like that, knowing we in here doing this?"

"Chill out, Banga! I didn't mean to scare you both."

"Fuck you!" Banga said.

"That's the problem! You want to fuck me, but you can't!" Meka laughed, as she headed to her room.

"No, I don't wanna fuck yo ugly ass!" he replied.

"I swear . . . sometimes it's like y'all married. At least y'all fight like y'all married," Ham said laughing.

"Fuck you, too, nigga!"

Damn, I do wanna fuck her so bad. Want to make her scream and climb the walls, Banga thought to himself. How does everyone know I want to fuck her?

"Hello, hello?" Ham yelled.

"Huh? Oh what?" Banga asked.

"Damn, you was outer space. I said I'm going over to hold down that other corner, so if you need me, ya know where I'm at."

Exiting the apartment, Ham went to the left while Banga went right to check on the other corners. Banga saw two people on the corner, so he walked up to them.

"Hey youngin's, what's up?" Banga asked.

"Just out here getting that money," one of them replied.

"So, what's your names?" Banga asked.

"I'm Jess. This is Adam."

"Sorry, I forgot your names. I see you both out here first thing in the morning. Y'all trying to move up the ladder or something?"

"Nah, just trying to get that paper anyway we can. My mom is out of work, so it's up to me until she gets another job. Feel me?"

"Yeah, I feel ya. Sorry about all you going through. How old are ya?"

"I'm 15 and Adam is 16."

"Damn, y'all don't go to school?" Banga asked.

"Yeah, but its spring break. School is a real good place 'cause half the students and half the teachers all use this shit, so school is very profitable."

"Well, keep doing a good job and you'll make that money. Here's some more for you," Banga said, giving them a Doritos bag full of little bags of dope. Then he headed off for the next corner.

TWELVE

After a long drive, Smooth finally reached New York and went straight to Jefe's house. Pulling up to the gate, a guard came out.

"Hey there. Smooth, right?" the guard asked.

"Yep, that's me!" Smooth replied.

Smooth drove up the long driveway until he reached the house. It was so big. Smooth was amazed every time by its size.

Smooth got out of the car, walked to the back, popped the trunk, and got the moneybag out. He headed up the steps where he was met by two more guards.

"Good afternoon, gentlemen," Smooth acknowledged.

"Yep," one said.

"Good day to you," the other said.

He was then escorted into the library as usual. Normally he waited until Jefe sent another guard to escort him, but this time he was amazed to see Jefe sitting there, reading a book.

"Hello, my friend," Jefe said.

"Hey Jefe!" Smooth answered.

Smooth walked over to where Jefe was sitting.

"Have a seat, my friend."

Smooth sat down.

"So, are you getting your usual 30?" Jefe asked.

"Yep."

"Raul!" Jefe yelled.

A moment later, Raul popped up. Jefe said something in Spanish. Raul picked up the moneybag and disappeared.

"So, did you read the book I gave you?" Jefe inquired.

"Nah . . . haven't had the time. But I promise I'll read it before I come back to re-up."

"I'll hold you to that, my friend."

"How is China?"

"Good for now."

"Tell her I said hello."

"I will."

Raul returned and said something to Jefe.

"Well, everything's good, Smooth. I will see you next time."

"All right. Later," Smooth replied. As he walked out the door, he was met by the two security guards and escorted to his car. As he left Jefe's home, he headed for the closet hotel. He was too tired to drive and needed sleep. He stopped at the Holiday Inn, got a room, and fell asleep as soon as his head hit the pillow.

* * *

Rebecca woke up the next day with a bit of a hangover. She got up and walked to the bathroom, opened the medicine cabinet, and grabbed a bottle of Motrin. She opened it and took three of them, and then took a shower. After the shower, she dressed and headed to the kitchen to start a pot of coffee.

"Hey there, buddy!" she said, as she petted Zorro. "Come on, let's go outside," she yelled, thinking the coffee would be done when they went back inside.

Once outside, Zorro led the way, smelling everything in sight and then pissing. After 10 minutes, Rebecca pulled the leash.

"Come on, boy. Time to go in and get coffee," Rebecca said, leading Zorro.

Once inside the elevator, she pushed the button for her floor. When the door opened, she was pleasantly surprised to see her brother knocking on her door and holding a bag of Dunkin Donuts.

"Hey there, handsome. You looking for a good time?" she laughed.

"Well yeah, donuts and coffee!" he said.

"I already got the coffee going and you got the donuts. So we good to go!" Rebecca said, as she unlocked the door. Zorro bounced all over the place, trying to get Spencer's attention. Finally, Spencer pet him, as his tail went wagging 100 miles an hour.

"So, how do feel this morning?" Spencer asked.

"I woke up with a splitting headache. It's been a long time since I've had a hangover. I did five years with nothing to drink, and since I've been out, I've only had maybe two glasses at a time. I should have known better not to drink so much, especially since I'm pregnant now."

"Glad I'm not pregnant, 'cause I'd go crazy without my beer and whiskey," he laughed.

"Yeah, well, I'm glad you're not pregnant, too. I need to make an appointment with a doctor to get an ultrasound. And to make sure everything's okay."

"Still can't believe I'm gonna be an uncle. You know I'm gonna spoil him rotten."

"Hell, I'm gonna spoil him, too."

"I can't get over you being a 26-year-old woman and not the 16-year-old girl I remember."

"Well, how do ya think I am? You're so grown up!"

"Guess we'll get used to it," Spencer laughed, while eating a donut.

Rebecca nibbled on a donut while she sipped her coffee.

"Ya know, I feel happy knowing I'm gonna be a mother, but some part of me is nervous and scared. Am I ready to be a mother? Will I be a good mother? It's got me going crazy."

"Sis, just relax. You're going to be a great mother," he said.

* * *

Working the corner was a good idea, Ham thought. He felt like a boss with all the crackheads begging him for a blessing.

"Dawg! I got $18, let me get a 20 piece," one of the crackheads asked him.

"Nah, bring me $20, and I'll give you a 20, simple!"

"I'll give you the rest when I get my check on the first."

"Man, get to stepping. You're holding up the line."

As the guy walked away, a beautiful, young girl came up to him.

"What's up, ma?" he asked.

"I need something. I only got $9 though."

Damn, this woman is too beautiful to be a crackhead, he thought.

"I can give you head, if that's what you want."

"Nah, I don't want head. I want that pussy!" Ham said.

"Okay, let's go down in the stairway to get some privacy."

"Lead the way!" Ham said, following her.

Damn, he couldn't believe his luck. She was so beautiful.

"Alright, this should be good enough," she said.

She got on her knees and started to undo his belt. He grabbed his gun so it didn't fall to the ground. Once his pants were around his ankles, she started to stroke his already hard cock.

"Go ahead! Suck this dick!"

She put it in her mouth and started to suck it. With his eyes stuck on her, Ham didn't see the guy walk up next to them until it was too late.

"You know what time it is, nigga? Empty your pockets," the man said, and he walked up on them.

"Damn, what the hell took you so long? One more minute and I would have had to fuck him," she said.

Realizing this was a setup, Ham grabbed the girl and put his gun to her head while they were talking.

"Yeah, drop the gun, nigga. Better yet . . . die!" Ham yelled, as he shot the guy twice in the chest.

"Now, get naked, bitch!" he told her. "Good, now bend over," he continued, while stroking his cock and getting it hard again. "Bend over more!"

Ham got up behind her and slid his cock up inside her in one fast move, causing her to cry out.

"Aggghh . . . please don't do this!" she begged.

"Shut up, bitch, and take this dick!" Ham demanded, as he slid in and out hard and fast. She cried out every time he slid in hard.

"You know you want this, bitch!" he said, as he slammed in again. Feeling himself about to cum, he sped up and slammed his cock into her hot tight pussy.

"Uggg. Here I cum bitch!" he said, as he came deep inside her.

After pulling out, he put his Glock to her head and blew it off. Heading back to the corner, he thought to himself that he was lucky he was at the corner where he was. Anywhere else, the neighbors would have called the police at the sound of a gunshot. But gunshots in that area sounded off every day

* * *

Ronny filled up empty chip bags with little zip-lock bags containing crack. After bagging it all up, he headed out to re-stock the runners. At the first stop, he pulled into a parking lot where he saw Prince Guru leaning up against his blacked-out Dodge Charge. He was talking to one of the runners. Ronny parked his Lexus and walked over to where they were standing. He gave both of them dap.

"What's good?" he asked.

"Nothing much. Just another day," Guru answered.

"I feel ya," Ronny replied.

"Shit . . . !" the runner said.

They turned around at the runner's reaction. A police car pulled up into the lot.

"Just chill. He just here to get his money," Ronny said.

Without getting out the his car, the officer pulled right up next to them and rolled down his window. Guru walked over to the car and handed the sergeant an envelope. He then walked back, as the police car pulled off.

"Paying him was a very good idea. He's been real helpful," Guru said.

"Well, here is a refill," Ronny said, giving Guru a chip bag.

"If you need more, just call. Well, It's been fun, but I gotta go," Ronny said, as he gave Guru dap and then headed back to his Lexus to go to the next spot.

But before he left, he decided to get something to eat. He saw a Wendy's and went to the drive-through. He then parked to eat his meal. Halfway through eating, he heard loud music through his open window. He looked a second too late, as a Mexican aimed an AK47 at him. Before he could even duck, the guy opened up. Ronny felt six rounds hit his chest and side. The car then sped off, burning rubber. Ronny's last thought was that he should have worn his Kevlar vest.

* * *

Smooth finally made it back to Florida and then headed for Banga, Meka, and Ham's place. A few hours later, he finally arrived there. Getting out of this truck, he opened his back door, took our four kilos, and put them in another backpack. He then went up to the door and knocked three times. A moment later, Meka opened the door.

"Hey sexy!" Smooth said.

"Ummm . . . hey handsome! Come on in. Banga and Ham are both gone. Banga should be back soon, though. In the meantime, let's go to my bedroom," she offered, as she grabbed his arm and basically dragged him to her room. Once they arrived, Meka began to take off her clothes.

"Get undressed!" she said.

Laying down the backpack, Smooth took off his clothes. Once he was naked, she told him to lie on his belly. As he did that, he felt her straddle him. Then he felt something cold being poured onto his back.

"Relax, it's only lotion," she said, pouring a little more.

She started to spread it around, covering his whole back. She then began giving him a massage.

He was getting hard just from the massage. After about 10 minutes, Meka told him to roll over. He did so, as his hard dick stood straight up. She straddled him again. This time she poured lotion on his chest and started to massage it.

Not being able to stand it, he told her, "Suck my dick!"

"Nope, just lay there and enjoy," she said.

"Damn it, you're gonna give me blue balls."

"All right," she said, as she lined up his dick and slid down on it. Her pussy wrapped around his cock and fit like a nice tight glove. She started sliding up and down slowly, making love this time instead of fucking.

"How's that feel, baby?" she asked.

"Feels real good."

Feeling herself about to cum, she moaned and picked up her speed a little. She bent down and started to kiss him as she came. She moaned into his mouth as she climaxed. Feeling her pussy spasm and her body tremble, he knew she just had a major orgasm. He rolled over and slowly slid his hard dick into her tight pussy. He pumped in and out nice and smooth until he reached the point of no return and shot his cum up in her. Now exhausted, he pulled out and laid down next to hear.

"Each time it gets better and better, she said.

Hearing the outside door open and close, Smooth grabbed his pistol while Meka peeked out.

"It's just Banga," she said, as she started to get dressed. Smooth got off the bed and started to get dressed as well. Then he grabbed the backpack and stepped into the kitchen where Banga was at the table counting money.

"Waz up, dawg?" Banga asked.

"Nothing much. Just stopped by to re-up you," he said, putting the backpack on the table.

"There are four keys there. Is that enough?" Smooth asked.

"Yeah, that's plenty. Just finished packaging up the last we had. Here, let me get your money," he said, as he went into the back of the apartment and returned with another backpack.

"Well, guess I'll get on my way," Smooth said, as he walked to the door.

"Call me if ya need me," he said.

"All right," Banga replied.

Meka followed Smooth to his truck. Once they were there, he put the money in the backseat and turned toward Meka. He kissed her, got into his truck, and then headed back to Miami.

THIRTEEN

Leaving the hospital, Rebecca headed to her car. She pulled out of the parking lot and went to the McDonald's drive-through. It seemed to her that since she found out she was pregnant she was always hungry. After getting her food, she parked and began to eat. She looked at the kids playing on the slides inside. Two of the children looked like they were having a great time. She watched them and imagined they were her children. But she did have to figure out what she would do with Smooth. At first, the arrangement was a really good thing. It was the best of both words: her, Smooth, and China. She really looked forward to all three of them being together. But now she wanted to have Smooth to herself—just her, Smooth, and their kids. But would Smooth go for that? Would he leave China? Sooner or later, she was going to have to give him the ultimatum. What was she going to do if he picked China? Could she raise a kid by herself? As she took a big bite of her burger, her phone rang. Without looking at the display, she answered.

"Vul-lo!" she said, with a mouth full of burger.

"Rebecca?"

"Yes, sorry. I was trying to eat. What's up? Are you okay?"

"Yeah, just wanted to let you know I'm back in town," Smooth said.

"Well, after I finish eating, I'm gonna stop by Subway to get a few subs for tonight. What kind so you want?"

"Get me the Italian."

"Okay. See ya when I get home," she said, ending the call.

After she finished eating, Rebecca then drove to Subway.

"Hey, what can I do for you?" the person behind the counter asked.

"I need a turkey club and an Italian sub."

"Okay," the woman said from behind the counter. After the sandwiches were made, Rebecca grabbed a few bags of chips and a few cookies. She then paid, headed to her Audi A4, and drove home.

* * *

After talking to Rebecca, Smooth tried to call Ronny again. No luck. Then his phone rang.

"Hello?" Smooth answered.

"Can I talk to Smooth?" an unfamiliar voice asked.

"I'm Smooth. Who's this?"

"My name is Big Mitch. I work for Ronny."

"Well, how'd ya get my number and why ya calling?"

"I got your number from Ronny. He told me if anything ever happened to call you."

"Well, why ya calling?" Smooth asked.

"Ronny's dead!"

"What? This better not be a joke. How? Where?"

"Somebody gunned him down in front of Wendy's."

"Alright. Go to his duplex and wait for me there."

"Okay!" Big Mitch replied.

Practically running out the door, Smooth headed to his truck and drove as fast as he could to Ronny's. When he arrived, he ran up to the front of the door as quickly as he could. Another big black guy was at the door holding it open.

"Smooth, thanks for coming so soon."

"You Big Mitch?" Smooth asked.

"Yeah, that's me," he said, as he stepped back to let Smooth in. Before they closed the door, a '95 candy-apple Chevy Caprice Bubble with 28s pulled up. Sue Rabbit got out of the driver's side.

"Made it here as fast as I could," Sue said.

"Well, let's get inside," Smooth instructed.

Once inside, Smooth saw about 10 other guys inside the duplex.

"So, what happened?" Smooth asked.

"Well, Ronny went to Wendy's and parked his car so he could eat. One of our runners just happened to be in Wendy's and he saw a car pull up. A Mexican guy pulled up beside Ronny's car and unloaded an AK47 on him. Then he took off.

"So, we still at war with those assholes?" Smooth asked.

"Seems that way," Sue said.

"Alright. It's open season. Run into any Mexican and take them down," Smooth ordered. "From now on, Sue, you take over Ronny's spot."

"Okay," Sue said.

* * *

Spencer and Tic, his right-hand man, parked in a car garage and waited for someone to come out. They had been watching the guy for four days now, so they knew his schedule. Six minutes later, the man walked out. Before he got to his car, Spencer and Tic got out and approached him.

"Hey Stanley," Spencer said.

"What? How'd you know my name?"

Before he could react, Tic shot him with a Taser.

"Alright, let's get him into the trunk," Spencer said. They unlocked Stanley's trunk and put him inside. Tic then climbed into the driver's seat.

"Remember, straight to the warehouse. I'll be following you," Spencer said. Tic pulled out and Spencer was right behind him.

Once they arrived at the warehouse, they pulled in and closed the doors. Spencer and Tic met at Stanley's trunk. They opened the trunk, and Stanley was now awake.

"Nice of you to join us, Stanley," Spencer said.

"Wha . . . What do you want?" Stanley whimpered.

"Get out of the trunk!" Tic ordered.

"Please don't hurt me. I'll do whatever you want," Stanley said, climbing out of the trunk. As soon as he was out, Tic hit him with the Taser again. He hit the ground hard. Tic and Spencer handcuffed his hands above his head and hung him from a cherry picker. They then chained his feet together. As Stanley came to, Spencer was standing in front of him.

"What do you want? I'll do anything, just let me go," Stanley pleaded.

"Okay, tell me where all the money is that you've been stealing from Code Red Security?"

"What money?"

"Wrong answer," Spencer said, nodding to Tic.

Tic took a pair of scissors and cut off all of Stanley's clothes.

"I swear I don't know what you're talking about!"

"The money you stole. Where is it?" Spencer asked.

Spencer gave Tic a nod. Tic took the scalpel and cut off one of Stanley's nipples.

"Okay, I'll tell you."

Another nod and Tic cut off the other nipple.

"I said I'll tell you!" Stanley begged.

"Okay, then start talking," Spencer said.

"I have two offshore banks that I use. I'll give you the account numbers and passwords. Just please let me go."

Spencer walked over to a table beside the cherry picker. It was covered with knives, soldering irons, coat hangers, a chain saw, garden shears, vice grips, and other torturous devices. There was also a laptop, which Spencer turned on.

"Don't try to lie to me or think I'm stupid! Now, give me the info," Spencer yelled.

Stanley then gave up all the information, and it all checked out.

"Now, tell me where the rest is, Stanley."

"That's all, I swear!" Spencer nodded to Tic who grabbed a pair of vice grips and held them against Stanley's nuts. Another nod and Tic closed the vice grips and ruptured Stanley's left testicle. Stanley screamed at the top of his lungs. Tic then used the grips on his left nut, which exploded under the pressure.

* * *

Once Sue was done re-stocking and checking out the last spot, he headed back to his dawg Guru's place. On the way there, his phone rang.

"Hello?"

"Hey, baby!" Cherry said.

"Hey yourself!" he replied.

"I just got home from my girlfriend's and wanted to see what you're up to."

"Just working. Why? What . . . you want to be up?" he asked.

"Thought maybe you'd like to come over. My sister's gone for the weekend, so I got the place to myself."

"Okay. When I'm done, I'll swing by.'"

"See ya then," she said.

Pulling into the parking lot, Guru was in his usual spot leaning against his Charger. Sue got out of his car and walked up to the three guys.

"What's up, Sue?" Guru asked.

"Yeah, what's good, Sue?" another asked.

"Nothing much. Just thought I'd stop by and shoot the shit."

"We were talking about the fight last night. Did you see it?"

"Yeah. That shit's crazy. Ronda Rousey was undefeated, and then bam! She got knocked out first round. I was totally poised. Good thing I didn't take any bets," Sue said.

"Yeah, a lot of people lost piles of money. Hell, I lost $300!" one of the runners admitted.

Looking over Guru's shoulder, he saw a Nissan slow down and then pull into the parking lot.

"Don't worry, I got it," one of the runners said, as he headed over to make a deal.

"Well, let me get up out of here," Sue said.

Back in his car, he headed over to Cherry's house. When he arrived and walked up to the door, he was met by Cherry wearing only panties and a bra.

"Mmmm . . . you look so good," Sue said.

"Well, come on in. Don't just stand there," she said.

Once in the house, Sue grabbed Cherry and kicked the door closed. He ripped off her panties and undid her bra. As she was standing there naked, he started to undress. By the time he was naked, his dick was hard as a rock just from looking at her. Before he could say anything, she dropped to her knees and grabbed his cock, pulling it into her mouth. She did her best to deep-throat his cock. But then he told her to stop.

"Stop! Now turn around and get on your hands and knees. I want to hit it from the back," he told her. She turned around and put her fat ass up in the air for him. He wasted no time and slid his hard cock inside her tight pussy, as he started to really give it to her until they both came.

* * *

"I'm going to the store to get some milk," Rebecca said.

"Do you want anything?" she asked.

"Nah, I'm good," Smooth replied.

"Alright, see yaw when I get back."

Once in her car, Rebecca headed to the gas station to get milk and some gas, since her tank was getting low. On the way, she went back to her inner battle. She asked herself if she should make Smooth pick her and his unborn child, or would she wait until the child was born. Either way, it was either her or China. She loved China, but she and her baby came first.

Arriving at the gas station, she pulled up to the pump, got out of the car, and went inside. As she was grabbing a gallon of milk from the refrigerator case, she heard the doorbell ring, letting the cashier know someone was walking into the station. She then stepped up to the counter to pay for the milk and gas.

Being in her own world, she didn't notice the two guys sanding in the corner.

"Freeze!" one of them said. Rebecca looked up and saw a young black kid pointing a gun at her. She dropped the milk. The other kid pointed a gun at the cashier, took the money, and then shot the person behind the counter.

"Fuck! Where did she come from?" the shooter said.

"Well, take care of her, Lucky. You know the rules. No witnesses!"

"I know!"

With that, Lucky shot Rebecca right between the eyes, blowing her brains out all over the potato chip stand.

FOURTEEN

Sitting on the couch flipping through channels, Smooth finally found a movie that was just starting that looked interesting. Out of nowhere, he got a craving for chocolate ice cream. He grabbed his phone, hoping to reach Rebecca before she left the store. The phone rang three times before a man answered her line.

"Hello?" the man asked.

"Who the fuck is this and why do you have my girl's phone?"

"Sir, my name is Steve Johnson. I'm a detective here in Dade County. May I ask your name?"

"Smooth is my name. But you didn't answer my question. Why are you answering my girl's phone?"

"Sir, I'd rather talk to you in person. Can you tell me where you're at?"

Smooth gave him the address.

"I'll be there in 15 minutes," the detective told him.

After hanging up, Smooth locked all the guns, dope, and money in his hidden safe.

Knock, knock, knock!

Damn, can't be the detectives so soon. Walking up to the door, Smooth looked through the peephole and saw that it was Rebecca's brother, Spencer.

"Hey Spencer," he greeted him, as he opened the door.

"Waz up, Smooth? Is Rebecca around?"

Smooth told him about the detective.

"Well, can I stick around?" Spencer asked.

"Yeah. Come on in."

* * *

Opening the door, Smooth saw two men in suits.

"Hey there. I'm Detective Johnson and this is my partner, Detective Smith."

"Come on in," Smooth invited, leading them into the living room where Spencer was waiting.

"Detectives, I'm Smooth. Rebecca is my girlfriend. And this is Spencer, Rebecca's older brother."

"Let's all sit down," Johnson said. After everyone sat down, Johnson dropped the bomb.

"I'm not sure how to say this, but Rebecca is dead."

"What?" Smooth asked.

"Rebecca and a cashier were both killed during a robbery."

"Where?" Spencer asked.

"The Speed Way right down the street," Smith replied.

"Did you catch the people who did it?" Spencer asked, one-step away from flipping out.

"No, but we have good pictures of them from the security camera," Jonson added.

"Can we see the pictures?" Spencer asked.

"Yeah," Smith said, handing them the photos.

"Do they look familiar?" Johnson asked.

"No, but can I keep these?" Spencer asked.

"Ummm . . . yeah, I guess. We have more," Johnson said.

"I appreciate it," Spencer said.

"I'm sorry about your loss. We will do everything we can to bring the killers to justice. We won't stop until we catch them," Johnson said, as he and his partner headed toward the door.

"If you see one of them, please call us right away," Smith said.

Closing the door, Smooth headed back to the living room where Spencer was waiting.

"Please, tell me this is a bad dream!" Spencer begged.

"I wish I could," Smooth said, with tears flowing down his face.

"Don't know about you, but I'm going to track these two down and kill them very slowly, making sure they suffer as much as possible."

"I feel the same way. Let's work together. I got a lot of resources."

"I have a lot myself," Spencer added.

"Then let's work together. If you find them, let me in. If I find them, I'll call you. Deal?"

"Here is a good picture of both," Spencer said.

"Thanks. Is there another for you?" Smooth asked.

"Yeah. Well, let me get working on this."

"If you need me, call me."

After exchanging numbers, Spencer left.

* * *

"Damn, I hate that fucking phone!" Sue exclaimed, while receiving a blowjob. "Yeah!"

"Hey, sorry to bother you, but I need you to get everyone together at Ronny's. It's very important."

"Waz up, Smooth?" Sue asked.

"Rebecca's dead. She got killed during a robbery."

"Damn, dawg! I'll get everyone and meet you there."

"See ya then," Smooth said, ending the call.

"Sorry, babe, but something important came up, so I gotta go. Not sure how long I'll be, but I will be back as soon as possible to finish this."

"Come on, Sue. Let's finish now!" Cherry said.

"No . . . can't! Too important!" Sue said, as he got up and started getting dressed.

"Remember, I'll be back as soon as possible."

"I'll be waiting!" she said.

On the way out, Smooth was already calling everyone to tell them to drop everything and get over to Ronny's. By the time he arrived at Ronny's, everyone was already there. Some people were smoking and talking outside on the porch.

"What's up?" one of them asked.

"Hey Sue. What's up?"

"Is Smooth already here?" Sue asked.

"Nah, not yet. So, what's going on?" another runner asked.

"Not sure. We will find out when Smooth gets here," Sue said.

Going inside the house, Sue found Guru at the kitchen counter drinking a beer.

"Was up, nigga?" Guru asked.

"Smooth's girlfriend, Rebecca, just got killed, and he told me to get everyone together."

About that time, Smooth walked in the house.

"Alright, everybody listen up. Two niggas robbed a gas station and killed my girl. I want everybody to look at this picture."

He passed around the picture of the killers.

"Does anyone recognize them?" Smooth asked.

No one answered.

"Alright, everybody get a good look. I got $20,000 for whoever brings them to me alive."

Now that got everyone's attention, Sue thought. Shit, hope I run across them myself.

FIFTEEN

❝ Hey boss! I know this is a bad time, but we are running short on product and need some," Guru said.

"I'll have some by tomorrow at lunch time," Smooth replied.

"Alright. Well, guess it's time to get back to work," Guru said.

"Yeah, it's that time," Smooth said, as he went outside and got into his truck.

After leaving, he stopped by his apartment to grab his pistol, coke, and some money. Then he went to Amanda's place. Once there, he knocked on her door. She answered the door after two knocks wearing nothing but boy shirts and a bra.

"Damn, man! Looking sexy as hell. You expecting someone?" Smooth asked.

"Naw, just relaxing. Come on in," she invited him, as she led him to the kitchen.

Once in the kitchen, he laid the bag on the table and sat down. She went to the cabinet, grabbed two glasses, and poured them both a rum and Coke. Walking back to the table, she handed him a glass.

"Here ya go!" she said.

"Thanks. I really needed that."

"So, what's wrong? You look like there is something wrong."

"Are you sure you want to know?" he asked.

"Yeah, I want to know. I want you to get it off your chest."

"Well, ya know my girl China is in prison, right?"

"Yeah, I know."

He told her the whole story about China and Rebecca. He then continued with how it was supposed to be the three of them, but that Rebecca got pregnant.

"So is that all?"

"No. The problem is she was killed today during a robbery."

"Oh my God! I'm so sorry!" she exclaimed.

"Why are you sorry? It wasn't your fault," he said.

"I just feel so bad for you and what you're going through," she replied.

"Well, let's change the subject. Here are four keys. Can you have at least two of them ready by lunch tomorrow?" he asked.

"Sure, no problem," she answered, as she walked over and sat on his lap.

"You know I'm here if you need me, right?" she offered.

"Yeah, I know. But the problem is I don't know what I need."

"I know what might relieve some stress."

"Oh yeah! What?"

She stood up, got on her knees, and unzipped his jeans. She reached in and grabbed his dick. She started licking the head while stroking it until he got hard. Then she put it in her mouth and started gently sucking on it, while using her hand to play with his balls. She started sucking harder, which caused him to gasp.

"Yeah, suck this dick. That's it!"

She started to deep-throat him while going faster.

"You know you love sucking this dick! Don't you?"

"I'm fixing to cum. You better swallow," he said.

He exploded deep down her throat. She sucked until she got every drop.

"Feel better?" she asked.

"A lot better!"

"Well, why don't you stay the night here?"

"Can't! I got other plans. Sorry!" he replied.

"I'll see ya tomorrow at lunch time," he said, as he headed toward the door. Once outside, he took a few deep breaths of fresh air before he got into his truck.

* * *

Damn! I'm out! Ham said to himself, as he pulled out his cell phone and called Banga.

"Yellow!" Banga answered.

"Hey cuz, it's me. I'm out and need more."

"You're already out?" Banga asked.

"Yeah man. They are selling like hot cakes. Damn crackhead everywhere over here."

"Alright. Meet me at the apartment."

"Bet," Ham said, as he put his cell phone back into his pocket.

"Hey, can I get a $20," a buyer asked.

"Nah, man. I'm out, but I'll have more in about 30 minutes. So, hang around, okay?"

"I will be here waiting, man. Are you sure you're coming back?"

"Yeah, I'll be back. Just chill for a moment."

"Okay, man!" the crackhead replied.

Back at the apartment, Ham yelled, "Banga, it's me!"

Noticing that Banga wasn't there, he grabbed a Coke and sat down to wait. After a few minutes, Banga walked through the door.

"Waz good, cuz?" Ham asked.

"I'll be right back," Banga said, as he headed to safe in the bedroom. He then walked into to the living room with more crack.

"Damn, man! They so many crackheads I can barely keep up, which is good 'cause the money is coming in."

"Yeah. I'm just glad you took it over. Look how much money we be wasting not being there."

"I'll be there until we find someone to take over."

"Well, I need to get back to work and so do you," Banga said."

"See ya tonight," Ham said, leaving the apartment.

Once back on the corner, he saw that the crackhead actually waited.

"Damn, man. What took so long? I been waiting for hours," the crackhead said.

"Sorry. Now what do ya want?" Ham asked.

"Give me a $20."

"Alright. Here ya go. See ya later."

Not even five seconds later, another crackhead popped up.

"Can I get a $10?"

"Here man."

Looking across the street, he saw a good-looking girl trying to cross. Once she made it over to his side, she walked up to him.

"I don't have any money, but I need a fix. I will do anything. I will give you a blowjob or have sex. I'll do anything."

Ham looked her up and down and liked what he saw.

"How old are you," Ham asked.

"Just turned 16."

"Damn, girl! You should be in school, not the streets."

"I know, but I can't change it. Will you help me?" she asked.

"Look, I'm gonna give you a $10. If you back here at 8:00 p.m. tonight, I will let you earn more. Okay?"

"Alright. I'll see you at 8:00 tonight. I promise."

Once she took off, another crackhead came up.

"Look, I don't have any money, but I got this," he announced, holding out a Glock 22.

"I'll give you a $50 for it."

"Alright, here," he said, as he handed the pistol to Ham.

* * *

"Pull up here," Spencer told Tic. Spencer got out and approached two black guys on the corner.

"Excuse me, have either of you seen these two men?" Spencer asked, as he held up the photo.

"What are you, the police?" one asked.

"No, but there is a reward for them."

"What? How much?" one asked.

"$20,000."

"Nah, ain't seen them, but I will keep my eyes open. How can we reach you if we spot them?"

Spencer gave them both his cell phone number as he got back into his car.

"Let's try another block," Spencer said.

"If something don't happen soon, I'm just gonna grab a few and torture them until I get those two," Spencer said.

Instead of getting out, Spencer just lowered his window.

"What ya need, playboy?" the dealer asked.

"Have you seen these two?" Spencer asked.

"Nah, man. Never seen them," the dealer said, as he turned around and went back to his spot. But before he could take two more steps, he felt something hit his back. Next thing he knew, he was trying to get up but couldn't move.

Getting out of the car, Spencer told Tic to open the trunk and help him. After popping open the trunk, Tic went around and helped Spencer. He grabbed the guy's legs, while Spencer grabbed his arms. Once they got him in the trunk, they both got back into the car and headed to the warehouse.

"That tranquilizer worked fast. What was it?" Tic asked.

"It's called Special K. But its real name is ketamine hydrochloride."

"Hey, it works, so that's good."

"First time I ever loaded the darts, I accidentally shot myself. I had to lay there for an hour until it started to wear off. Wasn't fun!"

"You actually shot yourself!" Tic burst out laughing.

"Keep laughing and I'll shoot you!" Spencer joked.

Pulling up to the warehouse, Tic pushed a button and the garage doors opened. Once they were inside, the doors closed. As Spencer got out of the car, he turned on the lights. The warehouse was huge. In the back was a two-room apartment. On the front side was the cherry picker, with two tables topped with torture devices, a computer, scanner, printer, and camera for making fake I.D.s.

After getting the guy out of the trunk, they tied his hands together and hung him from the cherry picker. Once his feet were off the ground, they cut off his clothes. They waited about 30 minutes before he began coming to.

"Well, hey there, princess. Glad you're awake!" Tic said.

"Yeah, real nice of you to join us. Figured you'd want to hang around and answer some questions," Spencer said.

"What's this about? Where am I?"

"See this is gonna be a problem. You are supposed to answer questions, not ask them. So let this be a lesson."

Spencer picked up a pair of scissors and cut off the man's right ear. The man began screaming.

"So, did you learn you lesson?" Spencer asked him.

"Yes," he moaned.

"So, let's try this again. Do you recognize these two?" Spencer asked, holding up the photo of the two killers.

"Nah, man," he responded.

"Thought you learned your lesson," Spencer said, as he picked up the scissors.

"Let me see if I can change your mind," Spencer suggested, as he cut off half the man's penis. After a minute of intense screaming, the man began to sob.

"Let's try this one more time. Do you know these two men?" Spencer repeated.

"I only know one of them," he replied.

"Which one?"

"The tall one."

"Who is he?"

"He's a known stick-up kid. His name's Lucky."

"Where is he?"

"Don't know."

"Well, time for another lesson," Spencer warned.

"No! No! I really don't know. But he sometimes hangs out at the club that just opened. Club Rage."

"Anything else?" Spencer asked.

"No, that's all I know. I swear!"

Spencer nodded to Tic, who took a scalpel and slit the man's throat.

"I'm gonna go check on some things. I'll meet you back here in two hours."

"Alright, boss," Tic answered.

SIXTEEN

" Glad you made it back. I was starting to think you forgot about me," Cherry pouted.

"I'd never forget about you, baby."

"Well, don't just stand there."

Sue stepped inside and closed the door. She was in the same outfit as earlier, still looking sexy as fuck. She grabbed his hand and led him to the bedroom.

"Let's undress you," she said, taking off his shirt. She got on her knees and began undoing his pants. Letting them fall to the ground, he stepped out of them. Next, she slid his boxers down.

"Ummm . . . is this for me?" she asked.

"Yeah, that's for you."

She put it in her mouth and sucked his dick until it was nice and hard. Then she told him to lie down. She took off her boy shorts and bra, and then she straddled him. She reached behind her and slowly slid down onto his hard cock. She started slow then picked up the pace. In no time at all, she came . . . and came hard. He flipped her over on her back and started to fuck her hard, until he exploded inside her. Then he pulled out and lay beside her to catch his breath.

"Damn! That was good. You always make me cum as I've never cum before. Shit, just thinking of you makes my pussy wet," Cherry said.

"Well, if you wanna know, you make me cum fast 'cause your pussy is so tight. It's so good."

"I'm getting so many feelings for you. I think I'm in love. Hell, you're all I think of."

"Well, I got feelings for you, too. I never had feelings like this with anyone. You make me feel so good," he said.

"Are you hungry?" she asked.

"Hell yeah! Famished!"

"Let's order a pizza," she said.

"Okay, go order it. I'll pay."

She headed out of the room. After a few minutes, she returned.

"I ordered a meat lovers deep dish and a ham and bacon for us."

"Sounds good, babe."

* * *

"Damn phone is always ringing!" Smooth said to himself. "Hello?" he answered.

"Ummm . . . is this Smooth?" the voice asked.

"Yeah, it's me. What's up?"

"This is Mac from Club Rage. Ronny gave me your number and said to call if there was ever a problem. Well, I been trying to call him for three days, and he isn't answering."

"That's 'cause he's dead. Got killed a few days ago. So, what you need?"

"I need a least five, but would like more."

"How many more?" Smooth asked.

"I'd like 10 total."

"I can do that. When you want it?"

"Tonight, if possible."

"Look for me around 10:00 p.m."

"Alright, see ya."

As soon as he ended the call, the phone rang again.

"Hello?"

"Hey bro, it's me, Banga."

"What's up, dawg?" Smooth asked.

"It's all good here. As a matter of fact, that's why I'm calling. We opened up another corner and we are having problems keeping up. We are really low and need some as soon as possible."

"Alright, I'll be there some time in the morning . . . before lunch. That good?"

"Yeah, that's good! I'll be looking forward to seeing you. I miss y'all like crazy!"

"Well, come on home. You know we got a spot for you. And you'll always be welcomed here."

"I know that. But for some reason, I feel like I belong here. I know it's crazy, but it's true."

"Okay, I gotta go. I will see you tomorrow," Smooth said.

"Alright. Later, bro!" Banga replied.

* * *

After taking off the leg irons, belly chain, and handcuffs, China was led into a room.

"Preston! Stand over there on the X and look at the camera," a guard said from behind the computer.

Click, click!

"Okay, now turn to your left. Good. Right there."

"Alright. Here is your new inmate I.D. I've turned it on so you can order from the canteen."

"Let's go, Preston," another guard said.

Leaving that building, China was escorted to her old unit. Once they arrived at the door, a sergeant walked out.

"Well, well. If it isn't the famous Preston!"

"Hello, Sergeant Butler."

"Well Preston, is it okay for us to put you back in your old unit? Those other two women were transferred."

"Yes, ma'am. Is there any way I can get my same room and roommate?"

"I think we can handle that. Come on!" the sergeant said, leading China to her unit. Once they got inside, the sergeant led her to her old cell and called her old roommate, Jenny, over.

"What's up, Sergeant Butler?" Jenny asked.

"You and Preston get along?"

"Yes, ma'am."

"Well, can she move back in with you?" the sergeant asked.

"Yeah. That'd be nice."

"Okay, ladies. Enjoy!" the sergeant said, as she turned around and left the unit.

"Damn, China, it's good to see you. You had us all really worried."

"Well, it wasn't something I planned!" China said.

"Hey, have you all eaten yet?" China asked.

"No. They should be calling chow any minute now."

"Good, 'cause I'm starving. Think the property room is still open?"

"Not sure, but it's worth a try."

"Because everything of mine is in property. I don't even have my damn toothbrush."

"Don't worry. If property is closed, we will figure something out."

"Shit . . . as soon as we get back from chow, I need to call home. My people are probably going nuts!" China said.

"Alright ladies. It's chow time. This is the first and last call for chow," a guard announced over the loud speaker.

"Let's go. We got chicken tonight, so it will be a long line," Jenny said.

"Yeah, better get towards the front of the line. Want it while it's still hot!" China said.

After getting their trays of food, they got drinks and sat down at a table to eat their chicken, rice, coleslaw, and corn bread.

"Mmmm . . . this chicken is good," China said.

"It would be better if we had some barbeque sauce."

"Hell yeah! That'd be heaven."

"Next time we will make some sauce out of ketchup, season packs, and sugar. I make it real good. Normally, I have it, but I didn't get money this month, so I didn't have the stuff," Jenny said.

"Don't worry. I got money. I'll buy you, cook!"

"Sounds like a deal!"

* * *

Feeling hungry, Smooth decided to stop by Roxy's and eat. Once he got there, he went straight to his table.

"Same as usual? Coke, no ice?" the waitress asked.

"Yes, please."

As soon as she walked away, Smooth's phone rang.

"Hello?"

This is a collect call from China Preston, an inmate at Lowell Correctional Institution. If you want to accept the call, press zero.

Smooth pressed zero.

This call may be recorded and monitored. Thank you for using G.T.L.

"Hello?"

"Hey baby," China said, in a sex voice.

"Damn China. You had me worried!"

"Sorry. Wasn't something I planned."

"So, what happened?" Smooth asked.

"I got into a fight and was beating this hoe's ass, when her friend came up and stabbed me three times in the back."

"I will be there on Saturday 'cause I miss you like crazy," he said.

"I miss you more than you could know. How's Rebecca?"

"That's something we will talk about on Saturday. I don't want to talk about her right now."

"That bad, huh?" she asked.

"Yeah, that bad!"

"So, how's Roxy and GaGa?"

"They're both worried about you and miss you."

"I will call them as soon as we are done."

"So, is your mailing address the same? 'Cause I got some pictures for you."

"Yeah, same unit, building, and cell. I got lucky to get my roommate."

You have one minute left, said the automated voice.

"I hate that!" China stated.

"I do, too. I wish they'd let us talk forever."

"Well, I love you and hope to hear from ya soon."

"I'll be there on Saturday," he said.

Thank you for using G.T.L., the automated voice said before it disconnected the call.

"I didn't want to interrupt your phone call 'cause I didn't want to bother you. But are you ready to order?" the waitress asked.

"Cheeseburger with onion rings."

"Be back soon," she said, as she walked away.

She has a really sexy walk, he thought. Wonder how good she is in bed?

"Hey stranger," Roxy said, bringing his thoughts back to the present.

"Well, China's okay. Just got off the phone with her. I'm going to see her on Saturday. Unfortunately, I have some really bad news for her."

"What's wrong?"

Smooth told Roxy about Rebecca's pregnancy, and then he told her that she was killed.

"So, like I said, I got bad news for her, and I'm not sure how she is gonna take it."

"Wish I could be there to help," Roxy said.

"It's probably best if I do it myself."

"Yeah, you're probably right," Roxy agreed.

SEVENTEEN

After getting into Club Rage, Spencer headed straight to the bar and ordered a rum and Coke. With drink in hand, he sat at the bar and looked around. A lot of females were dancing. One in particular caught his eye. She was in her early 20s, and she was wearing tight Daisy Duke shorts and a tight spaghetti-strap shirt. Her hard nipples were popping out. She was sexy as hell.

She looked over at him. She started walking over to him, staring at him straight in his eyes.

"Hey handsome. You by yourself?" she asked.

"Not now that you're here. Can I buy you a drink?"

"Yeah, Fireball!"

Spencer ordered from the bar, and her drink was delivered right away.

"So what's a beautiful woman like you doing here by yourself?"

"My boyfriend slept with my sister, so fuck them both!"

"He must be blind and stupid!" he replied.

"So, you know how to dance?" she asked.

"Yep. You want to?"

"Hell yeah!" she said, as she set down her drink, grabbed him, and led him to the dance floor, while

Whistle by Flo Rida was blasting through the speakers. They began to dance and she bumped and grinded all over him, getting his dick hard as a rock. The whole time he was dancing around, he kept an eye out for the guy named Lucky. After three more song, Spencer told her that he needed to take a break, so they returned to their seats and ordered more drinks.

"So, do you come here often?" he asked.

"For the last month, yeah!" she replied.

"Do you happen to know a dude named Lucky?"

"No, but you see that guy in the red shirt?"

"Yeah, I see him."

"Ask him. He knows every person here."

"Okay, I'll be right back."

"I'll be waiting," she grinned up at him.

Walking over to the guy in the red shirt, Spencer advanced slowly, trying to keep from spooking him or putting up his defenses.

"What's up? What can I do you for?" he asked.

"Do you know where I can find Lucky at?" Spencer asked.

"No," he quickly answered, but with a spark, that he definitely knew him.

"Alright. If you see him, tell him Spencer is looking for him."

"I will!" the guy said.

Spencer walked back over to the girl, but he kept tabs on the guy in the red shirt.

"Sorry about that!"

"No problem . . . Samantha!"

"Samantha?"

"Yes, Samantha. That's my name, since you forgot to ask," she joked.

"Well, my name is a secret, but everyone calls me Spencer."

* * *

"Mac, it's me, Smooth. I'm at your back door."

"I'll have one of my men open the door," Mac said.

Two minutes later, the back door was opened by a big-ass motherfucker. Bigger than anyone he had ever seen.

"Fe, Fi, Fo, Fum . . . what tree did you fall from?"

"Funny! Now let's go!" he said.

Stepping into Mac's office, Smooth laid down the bag of coke on his desk.

"Sorry about Ronny," Mac said.

"Hey, it's the life we live."

"Still, he was a good dude."

"Well, here are the 10. Let me know when you need more."

"Your money's right here," Mac told Smooth, pointing to a chair.

"Thanks."

"You staying to party?" Mac asked.

"Yeah. As soon as I put this in my truck."

Mac told the huge guy to hold the door. Once Smooth ran the money out to his truck, he returned.

"Thanks for holding the door," Smooth told the guy, as he headed to the V.I.P. section. He was ready to get his party on."

Once in the V.I.P. section, he ordered a bottle of rum and started checking out all the women. To his surprise, he saw Spencer dancing with a thick white girl. When the waitress brought over his bottle of rum, he ordered another one and had it sent over to Spencer. When Spencer received the bottle, he looked around and saw Smooth, who waved him over.

When Spencer and his girl got there, Smooth said, "It's a surprise to see you here."

"Nah, I do business here. So, it's a surprise to see you here."

Spencer leaned in and quietly told Smooth, "I had a tip that the guy named Lucky hangs out here."

"Well, you better believe I will keep my eyes open. Relax and enjoy the V.I.P. area. I'm gonna go get me a date," Smooth said, seeing a beautiful redbone in tight Miss Me jeans and a belly shirt.

"Hey there!" he said, walking up to her.

"My name's Smooth," he said, holding out his hand for her to shake.

"I'm Candy," she answered.

"Well, Candy. Can I buy you a drink?"

"Screwdriver with ice," she replied.

After getting her drink, Smooth told her to follow him to the V.I.P. section.

"Oh my God!" We are going to V.I.P.?"

"Yep. V.I.P."

"Are you famous?" she asked.

"No, I just happen to be friends with the owner."

"I have never been to V.I.P."

"Well, nothing but the best for a beautiful woman like you."

"So, you think I'm beautiful?"

"No, I don't think you're beautiful."

"What?"

"I don't think you're beautiful, 'cause I know for a fact that you're beautiful!"

Her face instantly lit up with a smile.

"Hell! You probably have a million guys approach you daily. So what made you pick me?"

"Well, I think cheesy lines are a waste of time. I like to get straight to the point."

"I like that."

"You also have that bad boy look," she continued.

"A bad boy look, huh? Well, what's a bad boy look like?"

"Sexy . . . has a certain walk . . . confidence . . . and don't care what people say or look like."

"So, you think I fit that profile?"

"So far! There are other things, too!"

"Like what?" he asked.

"Ummm . . . knows what he wants and won't stop until he gets it. Really good in bed. And has lots of secrets."

"Yeah, I pretty much fit that," he smiled.

"See . . . confident!"

"So, I'm a bad boy. What about you? What would you label yourself?"

"A sucker for a bad boy. I never learn!" she laughed.

"Well, I can see you're not a good girl. But you'll work," he played.

"I can pretend!" she joked.

"Well, why don't we get out of here, so I can corrupt you!"

"Let's go!" she said.

"Did you drive here?" he asked.

"Nope, took a cab."

"Okay. I got a car. No need to call a cab. So, your place or mine?" he asked.

"Mine, so you won't have to take me home in the morning."

* * *

At exactly 8:00 p.m., Ham saw the young girl crossing the street.

"Told ya I'd be back," she said.

"So you WERE serious?" he asked.

"Serious about earning more crack?"

"Yeah, I'd do about anything with you."

"My name's Ham," he said, holding his hand out.

"My name is Tina," she replied, shaking his hand.

"Well, follow me back to my spot."

Ham took off and headed to the apartment. He was really looking forward to this pussy. Once they got to his place, he led her into his room. Closing the door behind her, he started taking off his clothes.

"Go ahead, strip naked," he suggested.

She then removed her clothes as well.

"Damn, baby! You're beautiful," Ham told her. He thought she was a real knockout with a really nice body.

"Get on your knees and suck this dick!" he ordered.

She did as she was told. She then put it in her mouth and started sucking. She tried to deep-throat him, but she couldn't take all of him.

"What's wrong? You can't handle it?" he asked.

"No, daddy. It's too big for me."

"Stand up," he said. "Now turn around," he continued, as he admired her body. She had big breasts, a fat pussy, and a phat ass. He couldn't believe his luck. "Get on your hands and knees. Better yet, on your back!" he said.

He wanted to see her face when he fed her his dick. Climbing between her legs, he looked into her eyes as he slid his hard cock into her tight wet pussy. She was so tight. The look on her face was awesome.

"Ohhh," she moaned. "It's too big, daddy!" she begged.

"Don't worry; it will be over soon, baby! Just a few minutes," he said, sliding his cock in and out until he was about to cum. When he started to cum, he pulled out and shot cum all over her belly.

"Damn, ma! That's the best pussy I've ever had. Guess I need to keep you around!"

"Really?"

"Really what?" he asked.

"I'm really the best?"

"Hell yeah, by far the best!"

"Feels like virgin pussy, but better!"

"Well, you're very large. I 'bout died when I see it."

Ham laid there on his back.

"Here, straddle me."

"What?"

"I want to fuck again, but with you on top."

"I don't know how."

"Don't worry. You'll learn."

After straddling him, she slid down on his hard cock. Going real slow, she slid up and down.

"This feels so good, daddy!"

"I thought you'd like it."

Her words turned into sexy little gasps and moans.

"Go a little faster and don't stop."

She did as she was told, and he shot his cum inside her pussy, just as she came. Then she laid back to catch her breath.

"Tha . . . That was amazing! That's the first time I've ever came."

"Well, get used to it with me."

* * *

On the dance floor with Samantha, Spencer had trouble keeping the guy in the red shirt in his vision.

"Let's take a break and get a drink," she said.

"Good idea. You're killing me out there," he joked.

"If you can't keep up with me on the dance floor, you're never gonna keep up with me in bed!"

"I will. That dude in the red shirt. What's his name?"

"Doug. Why?" she asked.

"'Cause I'm looking for a friend and Doug knows him."

"Oh well, that's not me. Do you want to drive me home, or do you want to stick around here?" she asked.

"I'm ready. Waiting on you, sexy."

He followed her outside and led her to his Camaro. He opened the door for her and then walked over to the driver's side. After getting in, buckling up, and starting the car, he turned to her.

"What you waiting for?" she asked him.

"I'm trying to read your mind since you don't want to give me directions," he joked.

"Oh sorry. I'm just nervous."

"Nervous about what?"

"I've never done anything like this before."

"We don't have to do anything. I can just give you a ride and leave. Or I can stay. Totally your choice."

"Let me think about it on the way. For now, head to 27th Street."

"Your wish is my command."

"Funny!" she laughed.

"So, Samantha, what do you do for a living?"

"You'd never believe me."

"Try me."

"I'm a stripper at Foxy's."

"I bet you're the best and get more tips than anyone."

"Why you say that?"

"You're beautiful, got a killer body, and are a great dance. So yeah, I'd say you're the best!"

"Ah, make a left here. Second house on the left."

Spencer pulled into her driveway and looked over at her.

"Do I stay or do I go? Completely up to you," Spencer said, as he watched her in deep thought.

"Fuck it! Come on in!" she said, as she opened the door, walked into the house, and turned off the alarm. "Let's go to my spare bedroom," she said.

He followed her to the back of the house.

"Strip down naked and then sit on the bed. I'll be right back," she said.

After removing his clothes, he sat down on the bed. She returned wearing a skirt and a button-up shirt. She turned on some music and started dancing. He got up to dance with her, but she held her hand up to stop him.

"Stay there and enjoy the show," she said.

Going back to dancing for him, she slowly unbuttoned her shirt and took it off, to show a red bra underneath. Then she stepped out of the skirt. As another song came on, she removed her bra and G-string, and walked over to where he was sitting on the bed. She could see he had a major hard-on.

"Ummm . . . uhhh . . . looks like my dance got to you."

"Hell yeah, now come fix it," Spencer said.

"Lay back on the bed," she commanded.

"No, you lay down and let me do mine."

"Alright," she said, as she laid down completely naked.

"Do you do coke?" he asked.

"Never tried it."

"Well, do you want to try it?"

"I'll try anything. Never miss an opportunity."

Spencer grabbed his pants and pulled out a vile. He unscrewed it and used the little scoop to pull out some coke.

"Here, just suck it up your nose."

She did and coughed a bit.

"You okay?" he asked.

"All good," she replied.

"Well, my turn. Lay back."

She laid back and he poured a little coke on her left breast, and he snorted it up. Then he poured a little bit on her right breast. He snorted that up as well. He then licked both breasts, not wanting to waste a speck of coke. He set the vile on the table beside the bed.

"Spread open your legs," he said.

She did so and he immediately moved in between her thighs to eat her pussy. He then climbed up and kissed her as he slid his massive hard cock into her. She moaned and gasped with every thrust. She was really turning him on.

"Ummm . . . I want it . . . doggy style," she told him.

Spencer stopped to let her get on her hands and knees, as he slid in hard and fast, causing her to scream out. Before he knew it, she was cumming again. He picked up speed, thrusting harder and faster, and causing her to really moan out loud. Spencer then exploded, shooting his cum inside her. He then had to lay down to catch his breath.

* * *

"Hello?"

"Miranda, it's me, Smooth."

"Hey stranger!"

"Are you busy this weekend?" he asked.

"No, why?"

"I gotta go out of town and wanted to know if you'd watch Zorro."

"Sure, bring him on up," she said.

"Okay, give me a few minutes."

After he disconnected the call, he went to the safe. He got the money he needed and then grabbed his FN Five Seven pistol. After that, he took Zorro up to Miranda's.

Knock, Knock!

After two knocks, she answered and said, "Hey, big guy!"

"Hey!"

"Not you, hard head. I'm talking to Zorro, so don't get it twisted!" she joked.

"Thanks for watching him. I'll be back on Sunday afternoon or Monday morning."

"Don't worry. Zorro and I will be okay."

"Then I guess I'm outta here."

Once he got to his truck, he threw the money into the backseat and climbed in. Before leaving, he called Sue.

"Yeah?" he answered.

"It's me. I'm going out of town to see China and to re-up, so you're in charge."

"Alright. Enjoy your trip. I'll see ya when you get back."

After hanging up, he started up the truck and headed to Roxy's to eat before he left town. Once at the restaurant, he ordered soup and rolls while he waited to talk to Roxy.

"Hey Smooth," Roxy said, as she slid down across from him in the seat.

"How's it going, Roxy?"

"Can't complain. How are ya?" she asked.

"Good. Fixing to drive up to Ocala so I can see China tomorrow."

"Give her my love and let her know I'll be up next week with GaGa."

"I'll make sure to tell her."

"Well, let me get back to work."

"Damn, Roxy, you need a break . . . a day off or something."

"I'll be off next weekend when I visit China. But for now, work calls. Later!" she said, as she walked away.

After finishing his meal, Smooth got in his truck and started for Ocala.

EIGHTEEN

Ten minutes before lockdown, China got two big cups of hot water and headed to her room. Her roommate was still watching television. China got the food out of her locker along with the two bowls. She crushed up the soup, poured hot water on them, and added the seasoning. She then put a bag of chili into the leftover hot water to warm it up. After she got all of it cooking in hot water, she opened some saltine crackers and spread cheese on them to go with the chili and soup. It was one of her favorite meals to make in prison.

God, I'd kill for some real food right now, China said to herself.

"Lockdown, ladies. Go to your cells," screamed the guard over the loud speaker. Her roommate walked in.

"You done or do you need something else?" Jenny asked, as she walked into the cell.

"Nah, I'm good. I already got water."

"Okay," Jenny said, as she closed the door.

"You really missed the end of that movie. You won't guess who the killer was."

"Who was it?" China asked.

"It was her brother."

"Seriously?"

"Yep," Jenny replied.

China took the warm chili out of the water, opened it up, and poured half in one of the soups and the other half in another. She mixed it up really well and handed a bowl to Jenny.

"Thank you, China."

"You're welcome. Here's some cheese crackers to go with it."

"I really appreciate it, China."

"You're welcome. Now eat before it gets cold."

"Good idea. Damn, this tastes good!"

"Not as good as real food, but it does the job and fills you up. And don't taste as bad as prison food!"

"Amen to that!"

After eating, Jenny wanted to wash the cups and bowls.

"It's the least I can do after you cooked and paid."

"So, how much time you got left?" China asked.

"About four years left. How about you?"

"I got a year and a half left."

"How long you been here?"

"Year and a half," China answered.

"Bet you can't wait. Got any kids?"

"No kids. Yourself?"

"Two little girls. I miss them so much."

"You ever been with another woman?" China asked.

"No, I haven't. Why?"

"Because I want to relax you and make you cum until you forget about everything. Even if it's just for a little while."

"What would you do?"

"I'd have you lay down naked and then I'd kiss you all over and eat your pussy."

"I don't know. I never had anyone eat my pussy before."

"What? You never had your man eat your pussy?"

"No!"

"Well, will you let me try it?" China asked.

"Yes, I'll try it for you."

"Okay, get naked and lay on the bed."

China watched as Jenny stripped naked. She was not built like Rebecca, but she was still sexy. China kissed one of Jenny's breasts and then took it in her mouth and sucked on it, while using her other hand to massage the other breast until both nipples were hard. She then kissed her way down until she reached Jenny's pussy, slowly licking her juices up like ice cream. Jenny moaned out loud. China used her hand to spread apart Jenny's pussy lips so she could get to her clit and slide two fingers into her pussy. China started to suck on Jenny's clit while finger fucking her until Jenny was shaking and gasping. She exploded and came all over China's hand and mouth.

"How was that?" China asked.

"Felt so good."

"Well, get up and get dressed. Maybe we will do more tomorrow night, but I have to get to sleep for my visit tomorrow."

"Okay. Thanks. I'll see ya tomorrow."

China lay down and thought of Smooth and Rebecca until she fell asleep.

* * *

Waking up in the morning, Sue got out of bed and went to the kitchen to put on a pot of coffee. After that, he headed to the bathroom to brush his teeth and take a quick shower. When he got out of the shower, he heard his phone ring.

"Hello?" he said.

"Hey daddy, it's me!"

"Oh, hey baby. What's up?"

"Nothing. Just wanted to know if you were gonna come get me for the night."

"So, you wanna stay the night with me?" he asked.

"Hell yeah! I wanna spend the night with you. I love waking up next to you."

"Alright. I will call you about 6:00 p.m. after I take care of business."

"Okay. See ya then, daddy."

Hanging up, he got dressed and went out to the car. He loved his Chevy Caprice Bubble. He got in, cranked up his custom radio, and headed to the trap house. He pulled in and saw Guru's Charger parked outside. He walked up to the door, and before he could knock, Big Mitch opened the door.

"Hey Sue, come on in," he said, as he stepped to the side to let him enter.

Inside, Sue saw Guru and three other guys. They were counting money, drinking, and smoking blunts.

"Hey Sue!" Guru said.

"What's up with you all?" Sue asked.

"Not much, just getting this money while trying to stay alive and out of jail."

"I feel ya, bro!" Sue answered.

"So, Guru. You already picked up all the money and re-upped everyone"

"Sure have."

"You the man!" Sue replied.

"I sure am!" Guru agreed.

"Well, how we looking on product?"

"We are real low."

"Smooth is out of town until Monday, so we gotta make it last 'til then."

"We will do the best we can, but damn it seems like crackheads double every day. Not sure where they come from, but they keep coming!"

"I know what you mean, but we can't re-up until Smooth gets back," Sue said.

"All the money's here!" Guru said.

"That's good. Put it in the safe until Smooth gets back and can pick it up."

"Will do, boss man!" Big Mitch replied, as he took all the money and headed to the safe in the back.

"I gotta piss," Sue said.

"You know where the bathroom is," Guru said.

After taking a piss, Sue said goodbye to everyone and left for his car. Once he got inside, his stomach growled, which reminded him that he hadn't eaten yet. He drove to a Denny's and sat down to look over a menu, as a waitress came over to this table.

"Ham, eggs, toast, and coffee."

"Alright, be back in a few."

In a few minutes, she returned with his coffee.

"Food will be here soon."

"Okay, thanks."

Sue pulled out his phone and checked his text messages. As he responded to the last one, the waitress showed up with his food.

"Here you go, sir. Can I get you anything else?"

"Nope. I'm good for now."

After she left, Sue ate everything and debated on whether to get more coffee.

* * *

"China Preston! You have a visitor," the guard said over the loud speaker.

"All right, China. Have fun!" Jenny said.

"I wish I could have some fun with him, but I don't think the guards would like that," China said, as she headed out the door.

Once she arrived at the visiting area, a guard led her to a small room and said, "You know the drill, Preston. Strip naked and put your clothes on the table."

After setting everything on the table, the guard went through it, making sure that there was no contraband.

The guard then continued, "All right, run your hands through your hair. Good. Now turn around. Spread your cheeks and cough. Now get dressed."

After dressing, she went into the visiting area where she saw Smooth standing beside a table full of food and drinks.

When he saw her, he couldn't help but to break into a smile. She ran up, wrapped her arms around him, and gave him a big kiss.

"How ya doing, baby?" he asked.

"A lot better now that I got to see you," she responded.

"Well, I got a lot of news for you, but it's all bad. I don't know where to start!"

"Just tell me and get it out of the way."

"Well, me and Rebecca got along real good. I see why you fell in love with her. Well, she and I were having sex. She got pregnant, and we were excited and couldn't wait to tell you."

"Oh my God! A kid?"

"Yes, but baby, Rebecca got killed a few days ago during a robbery."

China had tears in her eyes and a very sad look.

"Are you serious? Is this a joke?"

"No, baby. It's all real."

"I have decided that I want to have kids. I want you to have my kids. I want us to get married as soon as you get out."

"I'd love that!" China said, now with happy tears in her eyes.

"Well, I didn't know what you wanted so I ordered a little of everything. I knew you like the pizza and chicken sandwich, but I don't want you to burn out on it."

"No problem. I'll take the bacon cheeseburger and the hot fries."

"I'll eat this then," he said, pointing to an 18-wheeler.

"So, how are things with your roommate?" he asked.

"Good! I ate out her pussy last night. Tasted good, too."

Smooth almost choked on his food.

"What's wrong? Didn't expect that?" she laughed.

"I'm just hoping you don't turn all lesbian on me."

"Smooth, nothing can come between me and you. And God damn it! I want some dick! I would get up on this table butt-ass naked while you fuck my brains out, but then they'd take away my visits. And I don't want to lose them 'cause then I wouldn't be able to see you."

"Speaking of visits, GaGa and Roxy are coming up next Saturday. Roxy's been working her ass off. So this little time away from work will do her some good."

NINETEEN

Back at the Club Rage, Spencer was at the bar looking around. He didn't see Lucky anywhere, but he did see Doug. He also found a thick white girl in a tight black mini dress. When she looked his way, he motioned for her to come over. Without a thought, she walked over to him.

"Hey beautiful, can I buy you a drink?"

"Yes, a Cosmo please."

He gave the order to the bartender. Once he was handed the drink, he turned back toward the young woman.

"My name's Spencer."

"Well, Spencer, my name is Tara."

"Nice to meet you, Tara."

"Same here."

"Do you come here often?" he asked.

"No, but every once in a while I like to treat myself to a night out on the town."

"Glad you decided to tonight."

"Why are you glad?"

"Because, I haven't seen a beautiful woman like you for a long time."

Blushing, she said, "Really? I'm not that good looking."

"So, what do you do for a living?"

"I'm a nurse. I work in the emergency room."

"So, you must see a lot of bad stuff?"

"Car wrecks, gun shots, stabbings, limbs cut off. You name it, I've probably seen it!"

"Do you like it?" he asked.

"Well, I guess I do. I like helping people."

"If I get shot, I'll call you," he laughed.

"So, what do you do for a living?"

"I'm a security consultant."

"Do you like your job?" she asked.

"Sometimes. I was in the army and fought in Iraq and Afghanistan. I did it for six years before I decided to go into private security. I was making $30,000 a year. Now I make $200,000-$300,000 a year, and I pick my jobs and work at my pace."

"Damn! I wish I had that job!"

"Don't you do side jobs?"

"What do you mean by side jobs?" she asked.

"Okay, anytime there is a gunshot victim in the E.R., you call the police, correct?"

"Correct."

"Well, sometimes we don't want the police to know, so we pay a nurse at least $5,000 to stitch him up."

"Are you serious? $5,000 a time?"

"Yep. Dead serious!"

"Well, make sure you call me next time."

Spencer immediately handed her his number.

"Put your number in my phone so I'll have it in case."

"Alright. My number is there. Unfortunately, I have to go. My ride's waiting on me, but call me some time."

"Alright. Later!"

After he watched her leave, he scanned the room to locate Doug. Finding him toward the back talking to a woman, Spencer just sat back and waited for Doug to leave.

* * *

Hearing moans from Ham's room was getting Banga hard. He didn't even know what she looked like, but she sounded sexy.

"Ohhhh . . . daddy . . . harder! Yes! Fuck me. Ohhh my God!"

After they finished and his hard-on went down, he hollered for Ham.

"What's good, cuz?" Ham asked.

Behind him, Banga watched as the beautiful girl walked out of Ham's bedroom to go to the bathroom.

"Just wanted to let you know I'm going down to Miami for a few days. So you're in charge."

"Alright. I'll hold it down until you get back. That it?" Ham asked.

"Yeah," Banga said, as went back to his room, pulled out his cock, and started stroking it. He imagined fucking his cousin, Meka. In his dream, she was moaning his name and begging him to fuck her. Before he knew it, he was cumming onto a pile of dirty clothes. Putting his dick back in his pants, he walked out of his room and ran right into Meka. Damn! Did she know? Could she tell what he just did? Why did he have a crush on the one woman he couldn't have? It was tearing him up inside. Every time he saw her, he got tongue-tied and got butterflies in his stomach.

"Watch where you're going asshole," she joked.

"Fuck you, bitch!"

"You only wish you could fuck me!"

"Look, I'm going down to Miami for a few days. Ham's gonna be taking care of shit."

"See ya in a few days."

Grabbing his overnight bag, he headed out to his car. After getting in and starting it up, he turned down the music so he could make a call.

"Yellow. It's me. I'm coming to Miami for a few days. Thought maybe you'd like to get together."

"Well, I'm out of town 'til Sunday. Have to re-up. But if you're still around by then, we can get together and get into some trouble," he laughed.

"I guess I'll get out of here then," Banga said.

"Later."

"After hanging up, he dialed Sue's number.

"Yeah?"

"Hey, it's me . . . Banga."

"Hey Banga. Been a long time. How's it going?"

"It's going good. Look, I'm in Miami for a few days and thought you and Guru would like to hang out."

"Hell yeah. Call us when you ready."

"Alright. Later!"

* * *

The world slowly returned to Doug who had a pounding feeling in his skull. Fuzzy reality came into focus. He tried to move, but no luck. His legs, arms, and chest were tied to a chair. He looked down and saw that he was naked. He tried to remember what had happened. He remembered going to his car and pulling out his keys, but then he felt a sharp pain in his neck. That was it. That was all he remembered!

"Glad you're awake, sunshine!" Spencer said.

"Looking up, he saw the guy that was looking for Lucky and he noticed he had a pistol in one hand.

"We are gonna play a game. I'm gonna ask you questions. If you don't answer, I will shoot you and then ask again. Real simple. Let me screw the silencer on. I hate that big echo."

"Ummm . . . boss!" Tic asked.

"What Tic?"

"Should we put plastic down?"

"Nah, we will just spray it down with a hose."

"Okay."

"Now to you. What's your name?"

"Doug"

"Doug what?"

"Doug Larwenski."

"Well, Doug. Remember last night, I asked you about the dude named Lucky?"

"I remember."

"Well, I'll ask one more time."

"I don't know him," Doug pleaded.

Psssttt was the only sound that was heard . . . until Doug started screaming.

Spencer shot him in his left kneecap.

"Quiet down, some. Quit being a baby. Now tell me about Lucky."

"I don't know him, but I have heard of him. He and his partner are jack boys. They'd rob their own moms for a dime. That's all I know.

"Where does he live?"

"I don't know, man!"

Psssttt . . . his yelling got louder this time, when his right kneecap exploded.

"Agghhhh! I don't know. Please, I need a doctor."

"No you don't! You need a grave dug!" Spencer said, as he double taped Doug right in the forehead.

"Have Johnson and Miller get rid of the body, and have them clean this up," Spencer ordered.

"Got ya, boss!"

Walking back to his Camaro, Spencer's phone rang. Looking at the display, he saw who was calling, and a big smile lit up his face.

"Hello, Samantha," he answered.

"Hey baby. You busy?"

"I got the night off and figured me and you could get together."

"Okay. I'm on my way."

TWENTY

Tired after all the driving, Smooth decided to stop at a Flying J truck stop. He needed to get gas, stretch, and get something to eat. Inside was a restaurant, so after taking a piss and stretching his legs, he stopped in the diner to get a bite to eat. While he was waiting for his food, he decided to make a phone call.

"It's Smooth. I need to talk to Jefe."

"One minute, please."

A few minutes passed.

"Hello, my friend."

"Hey Jefe, I'm in town and would like 30 of those things. Is that possible?"

"Yes, for you, my friend, it's possible."

"Give me an hour, and I'll be there."

"I'll be waiting, my friend."

As soon as he put his phone away, the waitress set his food down on the table.

"Anything else?"

"No. Thank you."

Smooth dove into his food, realizing he was starving. When he finished his meal, he left a good tip and then hit the road again.

* * *

Pulling up after passing through the security gate, there were the two usual guards at the door. When he got out of his truck, Smooth grabbed the backpack from his back seat.

"Hello fellows. How's your day?" he asked the guards.

As usual, they didn't answer.

"Follow me," one of them said.

Smooth followed him into the library.

"Wait here! Jefe will be here shortly," the guard told him.

Reaching into his backpack, he pulled out Jefe's book. It was really good. He hoped Jefe had more like it.

"Well, hello my friend."

"Hello Jefe!"

"Ah, I see you got my book. Did you like it?"

"Yeah. It was awesome. Any chance I can get another one?"

"Sure," Jefe responded, as he walked over to the bookshelves.

"Ummm . . . let's see. Okay, here is one you might like," Jefe told him, handing Smooth a book while grabbing still another one.

"Time is Money by Silk White."

"Thanks Jefe."

"Here is your money, Jefe," Smooth said, pointing to the backpack on the couch.

"Raul!" Jefe yelled.

A few moments later, Raul came in. He and Jefe spoke in Spanish. Raul took the money and then left.

"So, my friend, how have you been?"

"Not good. I miss China so much, and on top of that, I had a good friend die. She was killed during a robbery."

"I'm sorry. It is always hard to lose a loved one. All we can do is stay strong and keep moving on."

"You're right, but it still hurts."

"I know. Believe me, I know!"

"I appreciate the book. At first, I didn't want to read it, but I knew you suggested it to me. So I gave it a chance and figured I'd read the first 50 pages. By the time I finished those pages, I was hooked and I couldn't put it down. So thank you!"

"You're welcome, my friend. Hope you enjoy this one. It's just as good."

"I'll be looking forward to reading it."

Raul entered the room and said something in Spanish to Jefe.

"Well, my friend, everything is ready."

"Okay, see you next time, Jefe."

* * *

Once he arrived in Miami, Banga called Sue.

"Yeah!" Sue answered.

"It's me. I'm in Miami. Gotta go see my mom and then I'll meet up with you all."

"Sounds good. Just give me a call."

Getting to his mom's house, he was nervous and excited. He hadn't seen her in over six months because he was stuck up in Martin County. But now that he could move around, he planned on seeing her a lot more often.

Knock, knock, knock!

He tapped on the door. He had a key, but he didn't want to catch her off guard and scare her. He heard someone come to the door.

"Hey mom! It's me. Open up."

The door flew open and his mom was standing there with tears in her eyes. He stepped forward and wrapped his arms around her.

"My baby boy. God, I thought you were dead or something!"

"No, momma. I'm good. I'm so sorry that I couldn't come home sooner."

"Come in. Let me cook you a good dinner. You look like you need one."

"That'd be great, mom. I miss your cooking."

His mom made fried chicken, collard greens, sweet cornbread, neck bones, and rice.

"Damn, ma! You really put your foot in that kitchen."

"I'm glad you liked it."

"I always love your cooking. Nothing better!"

"So, how long you staying?"

"I'll be here a few days. Then I gotta get back to Martin County. But I promise I will visit a lot more. I've missed you like crazy."

"I've missed you too, baby boy!"

"Tried calling a few times, but it kept saying it was disconnected."

"Yeah. Prices on rent went up, so I can't afford a phone anymore."

"I'm gonna get you a cell phone and I'll pay the bill. That way I know for a fact we can stay in touch."

"That'd be nice, but I don't know how to work those things."

"You'll learn. It's not that hard."

After a few hours of talking and catching up, Banga figured he'd go see his friends.

"Look, ma, I'm gonna go catch up on things with a few friends, but I will be back first thing in the morning, like around 9:00 a.m. We gonna go out and have fun."

"I'll be ready. Don't forget about me."

"I'd never forget about you."

"Alright. Go have fun with your friends."

Leaving his mom's apartment, he called Sue.

"Hey nigga, it's me."

"Waz up, Banga?"

"We ready to party?"

"Yep. Me and Guru will be waiting on ya at the trap house."

"See you in a few then."

Pulling up to the duplex, he saw Sue and Guru on the front porch. He parked next to Guru's Charger, got out, and walked up the porch.

"Waz up?" he asked the two as he gave them dap.

"Nice to see ya," Sue said.

"You ready to party?" Guru asked.

"Yeah. Hell yeah!"

"Alright. I'm driving," Guru said, as all three of them jumped into his Charger.

"Nice ride!" Banga said.

"Yeah, it's my baby. Bought it brand new, blacked it out, put on new tires, and supped-up the engine."

"So, where we going?" Banga asked.

"Foxy Ladies on 79th," Guru replied."

* * *

Finally, back in Florida, Smooth decided to stop at Ham and Meka's place. He knew that Banga wasn't there, but Meka would be. He thought of her bringing a smile to his face. He had begun really enjoying his visits with her. Pulling up to their apartment, he saw Meka talking to some fine-ass redbone chick. But Meka looked sexy. Getting out of his truck, he walked over the girls.

"Hey Meka!"

"Sorry, but Banga's not here."

"I know. But I came to see you, not him."

"Smooth, this is my friend, Tisa."

"Nice to meet you, Tisa."

"Well, Tisa, I'll catch up with you in a little bit."

"Alright, girl," Tisa said, as she walked away, giving Smooth one last look.

"So, you really came here to see me?"

"Yes, I did. Is that hard to believe?"

"I guess not!"

"Well, are we gonna go inside? Or do you want to stay out here?"

Once inside, Smooth took Meka in his arms and kissed her.

"Damn, you taste good! Can't wait to taste the rest of you."

Smooth picked her up and carried her into the bedroom. He used his foot to close the door behind them.

"Take off your clothes for me."

He started to undress himself while watching her. Once they were finished, he looked her up and down from head to toe.

"Damn, you're beautiful."

"Yeah, right!"

He grabbed her and pushed her to the bed. He then spread open her legs and started to eat her pussy, licking it up like ice cream while he finger-fucked her. After she came, he told her to get on her knees. He got her turned over with her fat ass sticking out. He reached down and finger-fucked her again until she was on the verge of cumming. As soon as she was ready to cum, he pulled his fingers out and slid his hard cock into her with one fast stroke, causing her to cry out.

"Damn, this pussy good!" he said, as he long dicked her. He almost pulled all the way out, but slid back in the whole way. He finally felt himself ready to cum. He fucked her harder until he filled her up with his seed.

"Damn, girl! Ya got that fire pussy!"

"Glad you like it, 'cause I love your dick!"

TWENTY-ONE

Waking up, Ham felt a warm breast on his arm. It finally came to him that it was Tina. He slowly got up, trying not to wake her. He took a piss, brushed his teeth, and went back into the bedroom where Tina waited butt naked for him.

"Hey daddy!" she said.

"You want this dick, don't you?"

"Yes, I want the dick, daddy!"

Walking up to the bed, he lay down on his back.

"Come suck this dick!"

She got up close to him, leaned over, and stuck his dick in her mouth. She sucked his cock for a few minutes until it was nice and hard.

"Daddy, can I ride your hard dick?" she asked.

"Yes, you may."

She got up and straddled him. She slowly lowered herself onto his dick, gasping for breath. Ham could see that she was in pain, trying to take all of him at once.

"Slow down. Take your time."

"Thank you, daddy. I love this dick, but damn it's big!"

She slowly went up and down on his dick and got used to the rhythm. She adjusted so she could take it all inside her.

"Yeah, baby. Ride it just like that."

"Okay, daddy!"

She rode his hard dick until she came. Then he rolled over and slowly slid in and out until he exploded and came inside her.

"Damn, that pussy good!"

"And it's all yours, daddy!"

"What do you have planned for today?" he asked her.

"I don't have anything. Why?"

"'Cause I gotta go hustle and I can't leave you here, but I want you to come back tonight."

"I guess I'll go home, so I can change clothes and shower. Can I get a hit or two before I go? Please daddy!"

"Yes, I guess you can. Here is a $20 piece. I'll give you more tonight. Meet me at the same corner at the same time tonight."

"Alright . . . 8:00 p.m. I'll be thinking of you."

After she left, he took a shower, dressed, and headed out for the day. Before he even got to the corner, the crackheads were all over him.

"Let me get a $20."

"Let me get a $10."

"I got $18, can I get a $20?"

"Alright, everybody chill. One at a time. Now, what do you need?" he asked the first one.

"I need a $20."

"What you need?" he asked the next in line.

"I got $18. Can I get a $20?"

"If you can find $18, you can find $2."

"But, it's all I got!"

"Okay, I'll let you slide today, but next time you better have the whole $20."

"Thank you so much."

"Go on, get out of here! Who's next?"

"I need two 20s," a woman said, holding out $40.

Ham took the two $20 and gave her two 20 pieces.

* * *

Walking into the club, Sue, Guru, and Banga went straight to the bar, ordered drinks, and scanned the room for girls. Sue was the first one to stop on one. As soon as he saw her, he struck. She was a white girl with long blonde hair, wearing a tight white mini skirt and a matching top.

"Alright, fellows, I found mine," he announced.

"Have fun, bro!" Guru said.

"I'm hoping I will," Sue said, as he walked away.

Once he reached the blonde, he locked eyes with her.

"Let me guess. You want to buy me a drink?" she asked.

"Yep, buy you a drink and then maybe a few dances," he replied.

"Okay, sounds good. I want a shot of Fireball."

He led her over to the bar and ordered her drink. As soon as the bartender took the drink order, Sue looked into her beautiful blue eyes.

"Name is Sue," he said, holding out his hand.

"My name is Hannah," she replied, shaking his hand.

"So, do you come here a lot?" he asked.

"Probably every other week. It's nice to let my hair down and get my party on every once in a while."

"I feel you on that."

"Do you come here a lot?" she asked.

"No! It's my first time here."

"What brought you her then?"

"Came with a few friends. Kind of a little relaxation thing."

"I normally come here with friends. But tonight I'm by myself."

"Well, you're not by yourself now."

"I'm not?" she asked.

"Nope! You got me now. Well, unless you want me to leave."

"Nah. You can stay for a while," she joked.

"Well, let me know when you want me to leave!"

"I will. Ummm . . . are you married?"

He held up his hand to show her that he didn't have a ring on.

"Nope! See!" he said.

Just because you don't have a ring, don't mean shit! You could be one of those guys who puts it in his pocket when they party."

"Here, hold my drink while I empty out my pockets," he said.

She laughed and said, "Okay, not married. Do you have a girlfriend?"

"No, I'm completely single. What about you? Boyfriend, girlfriend, husband?"

"I'm totally single."

"So, what about that dance?"

"Let's go!" she said, putting her drink down on the bar. He did the same and followed her. At first, it was a slow dance. The next song was a fast one. Before he knew it, he was bumping and grinding. Enjoying the dance, he let her do her thing, while he just followed. She could really bump and grind, he thought.

Turning around, Hannah leaned into Sue, grabbed his hard dick, and playfully nibbled on his hear.

"Feels like someone is enjoying this dance!" she told him.

"Yeah. Both of us enjoy it," he joked

"I can tell," she said, squeezing his cock.

"So, are you just gonna play, or do you wanna go somewhere private?"

"Let's go somewhere more private."

"Do you have a car? 'Cause I came here with my friends, remember?"

"Yes, I remember. And yes, I have a car."

"Okay, let me tell them I'm outta here!"

Looking around, he spotted Guru. He headed over to him with Hannah following him. Once he got to Guru, he gave him dap.

"I'm outta here, bro!" he said.

"Alright. Be easy and enjoy yourself," Guru said.

Turning to Hannah, he said, "Lead the way, beautiful!"

Outside, she pushed a button and pointed it at a brand-new Chevy Colorado 271.

"Damn, where'd you hide that?" he asked.

"In my bra!" she laughed.

"This is a real nice truck," he said.

"It's my baby. Did have an F150, but I saw this, test-drove it, and fell in love. What about you? Do you have a truck?"

"No. I got a candy apple '95 Chevy Caprice on 28s."

"A gangsta car, huh?"

"I'd prefer pimp mobile," he laughed.

"Get in," she said. She put the key in the ignition, started up the truck, and cranked the radio. It had a kicking system.

She turned down the radio and said, "Okay, we got two choices. One, we go straight to my house, or two, you go get your car so you'll be able to leave if you want to."

"I'm not gonna just leave, but I'd like to have my car close to me."

"Okay, where am I going?"

He gave her directions. Once there, he got out.

"I'll follow you, okay?" he said.

"Good," she replied.

They finally reached a really nice area.

Gotta have money to live her, Sue told himself. After parking in the driveway behind her truck, he got out.

He whistled and followed her to the front door.

"So, are you famous or a kingpin?"

"Neither. I'm what they call a trust fund baby. But I have a fashion design company."

"What's the name?"

"We make specialty, custom design clothes, shoes, and blinds."

"Sounds like fun. Can you custom-design me a suit?"

"Like totally!"

"Might need your services someday."

"Well, I need yours right now, so come on!"

She grabbed his arm and pulled him upstairs into a bedroom.

"Let's go. Undress!"

"Before he was halfway done undressing, she was already butt naked. After he was done, she led him to the master bath. Once there, she turned the shower on.

"Let's shower. I love shower sex."

In the tub, she grabbed the soap and soaped him all up. She then washed away the suds. She handed him the soap, and he washed her entire body. He then slid two fingers into her pussy.

"Mmmm . . ." she moaned.

Turning her around, he had her bent over the side, and then he lined up his cock and thrust into her. She cried out at the sudden thrust. He worked his way in and out, causing her to cry out each time. She was not tight, but she wasn't loose either. She felt like she was custom-made for hm. When he got close to cumming, he pulled out of her pussy. He then stroked his dick a few time, and shot his cum all over her ass.

TWENTY-TWO

Smooth finally got back to Miami. It was only 10:30, so he figured he'd holla at Sue and the guys. So he called him.

"Hello?" Sue answered.

"Hey Sue. It's me. What you all doing?"

"Was at the club, but caught me a babe, so I'm at her place."

"Okay, I'll get with you tomorrow."

"Later."

He dialed another number

"Yellow."

"Banga, it's me. What's up?"

"Just fixing to leave the club."

"Alright. I'll holla at your tomorrow."

Well, guess I'm stuck alone for the night. Go ahead and head home, he said to himself.

Then an idea popped into his head. Smooth made a U-turn. He put four keys into a backpack, headed to the apartment, and knocked. Amanda opened the door wearing sweat pants and a wife beater. She was looking sexy as fuck.

"Hey there, come on in!" she said, as she stepped aside to let him in.

"I didn't wake you, did I?"

"No. I was watching TV. What's up?"

"Two things. Number one . . . I wanted to see you. And number two is I need you to hook up a few things for me."

"Alright," she took the bag and put it on the cabinet. While her back was to him, he stepped up, wrapped his hands around her, and started to nibble on her ears and kiss her neck. He used one hand to tease her breast, while he took the other and slid it down into her sweat pants.

"Mmmm . . . no panties, huh?"

"No," she gasped out.

His dick got hard just hearing her breathe. He pulled his hand off her breast to unbuckle his pants and pull his dick out. He used one hand to play with her clit, while holding her with his other. She threw her ass back, trying to get all of him.

"Mmmm . . . damn, you feel good inside of me!" she moaned.

"Well, it feels real good inside of you!"

"Uggg . . . . I'm fixing to cum!" she let out a loud scream, as she came. Smooth came inside her at the same time.

"Damn, that was good!" she said.

"Yep, just what the doctor ordered," he joked.

Pulling her sweat pants up, she headed to the back on the apartment.

"Give me one minute," she said, as she walked away.

A few minutes later she returned to the kitchen, walked to a cabinet, and took out two glasses to make them rum and Cokes. After pouring the drinks, she handed one to Smooth.

"Thanks!"

"You're welcome. Now, what did ya bring me?"

"Four. Need at least two tomorrow."

"I can handle that."

"That's because you're the best!"

"Yeah, yeah . . . I will have you two and maybe three by lunch time tomorrow."

"That'd be great!"

"I see you're not wearing the vest I gave you. Why not?"

"Slipped my mind. Sorry."

"I told you to always wear that bullet-proof vest. Only takes one bullet when you are caught without it. One time slipping and bam!"

"I'm sorry. You're right! Can't believe I forgot it."

"Make sure you don't slip again. This is a deadly game and everyone wants to win. They would kill their mom to get that top spot!"

"Believe me, I know what you mean. I won't forget again."

"Good! Now let me get to work."

"I'll be here around noon tomorrow."

"See ya then."

Smooth headed out the door and back to his truck. He was thinking about how bad he slipped up by not wearing his bulletproof best. Amanda was right. It would only take one time and he could be killed. He couldn't slip up any more. Just then, he remembered that he didn't call Jefe, so he grabbed his phone.

"Hello?"

"Yes, I need to talk to Jefe. Tell him it's Smooth."

"Please hold on a minute."

After a few minutes, Jefe came on the phone.

"Hello?"

"Hey Jefe. Wanted to let you know I made it back to Miami."

"Alright, my friend. I'll talk to you again later."

"Later," Smooth said, as he ended the call.

After deciding it was too late to go to Miranda's to pick up Zorro, he decided to just go to bed.

* * *

"Alright guys, you know what time it is!" Spencer said to his three men. The three had shown loyalty and respect every time. They had all been battle-tested, so Spencer knew they wouldn't freeze up when the bullets flew.

"Johnson, go in the back. Miller, you cover him. Tic and I will do the front. Remember … tranquilize the kids and wife only. Taser the guy. We need him awake and ready to talk. Don't need him doped up. Everybody good?"

After they all returned with a thumbs up sign, he pulled his ski mask over his face.

"Masks on. Green light. Let's have us some fun!"

Everybody pulled down their masks and headed to their spots.

Spencer tried the front door. It was unlocked. He slowly turned the door handle and pushed open the door, stepping into the living room.

"Clear!" Spencer said.

They walked through a hallway and into the kitchen. There were two doors on the left and two on the right. After checking on two of the doors, there was a loud boom.

"Shit! We got gun shots!" He hurried to the kitchen where the noise came from. Both little girls and the wife were on the floor, as were both Johnson and Adam, the man they came for.

"What the fuck!" Spencer asked.

"We came in and hit the girl, and then a fucking pistol came out from under the table. Before I could Taser him, he shot Johnson."

"How bad, buddy?" Spencer asked.

"Not sure, but it hurts like a bitch!"

"Alright. Miller . . . help Johnson to the car. Tic . . . help me get this guy to the car. Outside they slowly slid Johnson into the backseat. Then they shoved the other guy into the trunk and Tasered him again just for fun.

"Where we going, boss?" Tic asked.

"Let's head back to the warehouse," Spencer said.

"How ya doing, Johnson?" Tic asked.

"Lots of pain, but okay other than that."

"Alright, Tic. Forget the warehouse I got a better idea. Get off the next exit and head to that Holiday Inn."

"Yes, boss."

After getting Johnson into a room, Spencer told Tic and Miller to take Adam back to the warehouse and chain him up. As soon as they left, he pulled out his phone and made a call.

"Hello?"

"Is this Tara?"

"Yes! Who's this?"

"It's Spencer. We met at the club."

"Oh yeah, I remember."

"So, were you serious about earning that $5,000?"

"Hell yeah! Why, do you need me?"

"Yep. Really need ya."

"Where you need me to go?"

Spencer gave her directions.

"Give me about 10 minutes."

While waiting, Spencer remembered how sexy Tara was and how great her voice was. Then his thoughts turned to his sister. He couldn't believe how they had never gotten caught before. Every drug dealer in the city was looking for them, as were the police.

Knock, knock, knock!

Spencer pulled out his gun and went to the door. Looking out the peephole, he saw that it was Tara's sexy ass. He opened the door and told her to come in.

"Glad you made it."

"So, what's up?" she asked.

"My friend got shot."

"Where is he?"

"In the bathtub, trying not to get blood everywhere."

"Lead the way."

Smooth noticed she brought a big backpack with her.

"Plan on going camping?"

"No! I just didn't know what you'd need, so I brought a little of everything."

"Good thinking. All right. Tara this is Johnson. Johnson, this is Tara, your nurse."

"Well, she's a lot better looking than the last one you gave me," Johnson laughed.

"Hey, that man saved your life!"

"Don't remind me!"

"So, what happened last time?" Tara asked.

"I got shot in the side really bad. By the grace of God, that man saved me."

"Okay, lean forward, so I can cut this shirt off," Tara asked. "Well, it's not too bad. It went in and out. Didn't mess up anything much. Tore some muscle. That's about it!"

"So, I'm not dying?" Johnson laughed.

"Not really. But you might feel like dying while I'm stitching you up!"

"Great! Can I get something for the pain?" he asked.

"What? Big bad man can't handle a few needles?" she joked.

"Hell no, I can't!"

"Good thing you'll never have to give birth to a kid!"

"So, can I get something for the pain?"

"I guess," she said, as she looked around in her bag.

Finally, she found what she was looking for. A needle and a vile. A few seconds later, she gave him an injection.

What is that?" he asked.

"Kinda like morphine. It will definitely kill the pain."

"Thank you," he said.

Spencer walked back into the bathroom and asked, "Is he dead yet?"

"No. He's alive and kicking!" Tara said.

"Okay. Then get your ass up and shower. We got work to do."

"That's not a good idea!" Tara suggested.

"Why not?"

"One, he's doped up. Two, I just gave him stitches so he can't get them wet. And, three, he has a lot of muscle tissue damage. He will have to be very careful the next two weeks, so he don't really mess himself up."

"Okay, clean up the best you can and get some sleep. I'll be back in the morning."

"Okay, boss!"

"It's the best I could do."

"That's alright. Here is your money. You earned it," he said, as he handed her the cash.

"Thank you, Spencer. Call me again if you need my help."

"Will do," Spencer said, as he and Tara stepped out of the motel room and headed to their cars.

* * *

"Wake up girls! It's work call. Everyone out!"

"Well, China. That's us! Time to go out to the wonderful recreation yard," Jenny said.

"Make sure the lockers are locked," China reminded her.

"Yeah, they locked. Let's go!"

Since they'd be going outside in the heat and humidity, China decided to get some Cokes and ice cream.

"Go get us some seats to the volleyball court, while I go and get us some Cokes and shit."

"Sounds good. I will be waiting."

In the canteen line, China was trying to figure out what to get for her and Jenny.

"Hey China," someone said behind her back.

"Hey Angie. What's up?"

"Just coming to check my card to see if my money's on it."

"Well, why don't you get in front of me. If your money's not here, I'll get you a Coke. It's so fucking hot."

"Yeah. I miss air conditioning."

"Me, too. I miss a lot of stuff I never thought I'd miss."

"Ain't that the truth!"

"Here, get in front of me so you can check your card," China says, stepping by to let Angie in front of her.

"Are you sure?" Angie asked.

"I'm sure. What kind of Coke you want?"

"Coca Cola."

"Next in line. Step up!" a guard announced.

Angie stepped up and put her card in the window. She had her card and receipt handed back to her, which meant there was no money was on it.

"Wait by the gate," China told Angie.

China stepped up to the window and handed her card to the cashier.

"What can I get you?" she asked.

"Give me three Cokes and three Klondike bars."

"Okay. Anything else?"

"Nope. I'm good!"

"Okay. Enjoy!"

China grabbed her stuff and headed back to the recreation yard. Angie was waiting by the gate.

"Here you go," China said, handing her a Coke and ice cream.

"Thank you so much! I owe you one," Angie said.

"You don't owe me. I did that from the heart. If you want to re-pay me, pay it forward! Give it to someone else that needs it."

"I will. But thanks anyway."

"You playing volleyball today?" China asked.

"I'm gonna try. What about you?" Angie asked.

"I'm hoping to. Why don't we pair up and call downs?"

"Sounds good."

"Go get us downs. Me and Jenny are gonna be up here eating our ice cream."

"I'll let you know when we're up."

China and Jenny enjoyed their ice cream and drank their Cokes. While watching the game, both teams were good. But she thought she and Angie could beat either of the teams.

Angie walked up and said, "We go next, so be ready."

"I'm totally ready."

"You sure you're up to this, so soon after your surgery?"

"I'm good, believe me! I'm good!" China said.

"Alright. We're up! Let's go," Angie said.

It felt nice stepping onto the hot sand. The ball was in the air. China jumped up to spike the ball.

"Point!"

"China Preston to Medical! China Preston to Medical!" a voice announced over the loud speaker. China put on her shoes and told Jenny she'd catch up with her later. At the medical building, she went straight to the officer's desk.

"My name is China Preston. Someone called me here."

"Yeah, Mrs. Taylor wanted to see you. Have a seat 'til she comes out."

After sitting down, China tried to figure out why she was called. She turned to the girl next to her.

"Hey, do you know who Mrs. Taylor is?" China asked.

"Yeah, she's a classification officer."

"Thanks."

"You're welcome."

The side door opened and an older woman in street clothes walked in.

"China Preston?" she asked.

"Yes, ma'am. I'm Preston."

"Follow me, please."

China followed her to the second door on the left.

"Have a seat. Now, I'm Mrs. Taylor, your new classification officer. I brought you here because some beds at work camps opened up, and you're eligible for them."

"What do you mean by work camps?"

"Well, you go to work every day, but you'd have to stay locked up at night. I hear they are really nice."

"Are there any close to Miami?" China asked.

"Hmmmm . . . let's see," she said, as she turned to her computer and did some typing.

"There is one in Loxahatchee."

"Okay, I'd like to go then. Anything's got to be better than here. So how soon 'til I would leave?" China asked.

"You'd probably leave on Tuesday or Thursday."

"Thank you."

"You're welcome. Just stay out of trouble."

"Don't worry. I will," China responded.

Back in the recreation yard, China found Jenny in the same spot.

"You won't believe this!" China said.

"Damn, you look like you just got dicked down."

"Close enough! They are sending me to a work camp."

"Wow . . . which one?"

"Ummm . . . Loxahatchee."

"That's great! You'll be closer to home, and you'll have a lot more freedom."

"I can't wait to tell Smooth."

"When you leaving?" Jenny asked.

"She said probably Tuesday or Thursday."

"I know I'm gonna miss you."

"Yeah, right. You'll probably throw a party the day I leave," China joked.

TWENTY-THREE

Waking up the next morning, Banga felt someone wrapped up around him. He slowly moved to get out from her. Too late.

"Well good morning to you too," she said, "Sorry, didn't want to wake you."

"It's alright. I needed to get up anyway," she responded, as she climbed out of the bed butt-ass naked. Not too bad looking. He could have done better, but he could have done a lot worse, too.

"Let me start a pot of coffee," she offered, as she left the room. He heard pots and pans banging. He got up, grabbed his clothes, and walked into the kitchen. He could smell coffee brewing.

"Nothing better than a nice fresh cup of coffee to start the day," he said.

"No? What about a blowjob?"

"Oh well. That's a good thing, too! You offering?"

"If you want me to."

"Well, I can never turn down a free blow job!"

He unbuttoned his pants and pulled out his dick. She got down on her knees and put his soft dick in her mouth. She started sucking it in and playing with his balls, until he was fully erect.

"Now, that's nice!' he told her.

"Mmmm . . . mmmm," she said, while sucking his dick. She was a pro, and he was about to cum real soon.

"I'm fixing to cum!" he told her.

She pulled his dick out of her mouth and used her hand to stroke his cock until he busted a nut and came all over her face like a porn star. Then she put it back in her mouth to suck it dry. She stood up, went to the sink, and grabbed a washrag and cleaned her face and hands. After that, she made them both a cup of coffee.

"I just sucked your dick and I don't even remember your name," she said.

"Does it make you feel any better that I don't know yours either?" he said.

"My name is Ginny," she said shyly.

"Well, name is Banga."

"Banga!" she asked.

"Yes, that's my name."

"So, is this a one-time thing? Or is it gonna be a lot?"

"To be honest, I'm not sure."

"What do you mean, you're not sure!"

'I'd like for it to go on, but the problem is that I don't live in Miami. I live in Martin County. However, my mom lives here, so I will be here a lot. But not all the time. So it'd have to be a long-distance relationship. Could you handle that?"

"Well, we can always try it and see how it works out."

"Here, let me take your picture. He pulled out his phone and took a few photos of her while she was still naked.

"Now, what's your cell number?"

She told him and then went to the bedroom. She returned with her phone, took a few pics of him, and then got his phone number.

"Oh shit!" he said.

"What?"

"I'm supposed to be at my mom's. I'm sorry, but I got to go. I will call you as soon as I leave my mom's."

"A mama's boy, huh?" she joked.

"Yep! That's me!"

"Alright. I will see ya tonight."

He ran to his car. He couldn't believe he was late. He arrived at his mom's and ran up to the door. Before he got halfway there, the door opened and his mom appeared.

"So sorry I'm late, mom."

"Eh, it's only a few minutes. At least you're here now."

He gave his mom a big hug and kissed her on her forehead.

"Let's go, mom!" he said, as he opened the passenger door for her and then walked around to the driver's side.

"Where do you wanna eat, mom?" he asked.

"Let's go to McDonald's. I could use me some egg and sausage biscuits, hash browns, and a hot cup of coffee."

"Then to McDonald's it is!"

After ordering, they sat down at a back table so they could see everything. As soon as he went to take a bite, his phone rang.

"Hello?" he answered.

This is a collect call from Jacob Spears, an inmate at Martin County Jail. If you want to accept the call, press zero.

Banga pressed zero.

This call may be recorded and monitored. Thank you for using G.T.L.

"Hello?" Jacob Spears asked.

"Hey buddy! Glad you called."

"Yeah, I got your letter, pictures, and money. I really appreciate it."

"No problem. How's your writing coming?"

"Got two books published, and I'm hard at work on the third."

"That's what's up."

"I got you and Guru in there, too."

"For real?"

"Yep."

"So, how is everything else going?"

"Finally got back in touch with my sister. She got married, so it's Amy McKinney now. Can't believe she's all grown up with kids of her own."

"Well, time moves on. And time stop for no one. Remember that! Also remember that if there is hope in the future, there is power in the present."

"I'll remember that. Hell, I might even put it in my book. Well, my sister, Amy, has been putting money on the phone, so I'm able to call every Saturday. And I love it. Ray Brown, the dude from Good2Go, has been a lot of help. He's even sent me books to read. I'm gonna give him as shout out in my book 'cause he's a good dude."

You have one minute left, said the automated voice.

"Alright, Jacob. Keep your head up . . . and keep writing."

"I will. Take care, bro."

"Ending the call, he looked at his mom.

"Sorry about that."

"No problem."

They both went back to eating. After they were done, they left and headed to the mall. Inside, he took her straight to the cell phone store.

"Well, what do you want, mom?"

"How 'bout that fancy purple one."

"Let's get that purple Samsung Galaxy 6. And let's get the case and charger for it."

"Alright! Anything else?" the clerk asked.

"No, we are good. Thanks."

As they left, Banga turned to his mom and asked, "Where to next?"

"I'm not sure. I don't usually come to the mall. I go to Wal-Mart."

"Okay, let's go in here," he said, taking her into the Gap.

* * *

Not believing his eyes, Guru turned around and looked again. He pulled over and grabbed his phone to make a call.

"Hello?" Smooth answered.

"Hey Smooth. You not gonna believe who I'm looking at."

"Who?"

"Lucky. The tall dude from those photos you showed us."

"Damn, where you at?"

"Gas station on 54th Street."

"Follow him if he leaves. Don't lose that mutherfucker!"

"Don't worry, I won't!"

* * *

Smooth disconnected the call and dialed another number.

"Yesssss," Spencer said.

"What the hell's wrong with you?"

"Nothing, I'm lifting weights. Why? What's up?"

"One of my men just spotted that dude, Lucky!"

"Where?"

"Gas station on 54th Street."

"I'm on my way."

"I'm on my way, too. My man is going to follow him if he leaves."

"Good. I'd hate to lose him."

"Me, too."

Smooth flew to the gas station. When he got close, he called Guru.

"Hey!"

"He's still at the gas station."

"Yeah, he is standing next to a brown car."

"Alright. I'm pulling in now. I see him. We gotta wait for Spencer."

Smooth got out of his car and went over to Guru. A minute later, Spencer's Camaro flew into the parking lot. When he got out of the car, all three of them met up in front of Guru's Charger.

"Alright, guys. Let's do this!" Guru said.

"Nah, wait. How we gonna do this?"

"I got a Taser and a dart gun. Here, take the Taser. Guru, be ready. We're going to Taser that other dude and I'll tranquilize Lucky. Smooth, you be ready just in case."

Smooth watched as they downed both guys. Then he walked over and helped carry them into the brown car.

"Guru! Take your car. Spencer, you take yours and I'll take their car."

"Where ya going, Smooth?" Spencer asked.

"I'm not sure."

"Follow me then. I got a perfect spot."

They each got back into their cars. Guru went in one direction, while Smooth followed Spencer to a warehouse. Pulling up outside, the doors automatically opened. Smooth pulled right behind Spencer. Spencer then got out and the lights turned on inside. Smooth was in awe of how large the building was. Spencer motioned for Smooth to pull up beside some tables, which were covered with blood-soaked torture devices.

"Told you I had the perfect spot. Let's get these guys out."

Smooth and Spencer got both of them out of the car. They tied up Lucky and hung him from the cherry picker.

"What about the other guy?" Smooth asked.

"Casualty of war!" Spencer said, as he pulled out a pistol and shot him twice in the head."

Now, we just gotta wait 'til this bitch comes to."

Spencer went to the table, grabbed a pair of scissor, and removed Lucky's clothing. After about 20 minutes, Lucky began to come around.

"Alright. You can join in or just watch. It's up to you," Spencer said, as he picked up some bolt cutters.

"Hey there, princess!"

"What the fuck! Who are you? This isn't funny!"

"You're right, it's not funny. But I'm gonna enjoy every minute of it. As a matter of fact, let's get started," Spencer said, as he took the bolt cutters and cut off Lucky's little toe.

"Aggghhh . . . God," Lucky screamed.

"Stop crying like a bitch! And believe me, God's not gonna help you," Spencer said, as he cut off another toe.

After he had cut off every toe, Smooth grabbed the bolt cutters and cut off Lucky's penis. Spencer laughed the entire time.

"Told you I'd enjoy every minute of it!"

Lucky was still screaming and crying, begging for them to stop.

"Now that we have your attention, who is this man with you in this photo?"

"That's Rob, my homeboy!"

"Where is he?"

"He's at his cousin's in Palm Beach. He'll be back tomorrow."

"Where will he be?"

"At his apartment."

"Where is his apartment?"

"On 79th Street. Building C. Room 6."

Spencer opened his wallet and showed Lucky a picture of Rebecca.

"You remember her?"

"Nah, man. Never seen her."

"You're lying. You two killed her when you robbed a gas station," Spencer screamed, as he picked up a knife and began skinning Lucky alive. His screams were music to Spencer's ears.

Finally getting bored, Spencer handed Smooth the pistol. He took it and, without a thought, shot Lucky in the head.

"Now, tomorrow we get the next one!" Spencer said.

"Yeah, tomorrow. That really was weird. It was sick, but I loved every minute of it!' Smooth said.

"It's a lot of pain for them, but joy for us. Some people don't have the stomach for it. I've seen people throw up at the sight of blood. But I've also seen guys who bathe in it," Spencer told him.

"Well, I'm not gonna bathe in it, but I'm not gonna run from it either. Is this some stuff you learned in the military?"

"Yes. Well, kind of. I shot a lot of people. Then I got into Special Forces and a whole new world opened up for me. We'd torture guys for days to find a foxhole or the Taliban. At first, I was just watching and then I started to join in. Just make sure you're up to it. Anytime you need a spot, let me know and I'll let you use this," Spencer said.

"Okay. Now what do we do with the body?" Smooth asked.

"I got a team of four ex-Special Forces dudes on my team. They take care of all that for me."

"Can I get a ride back to my car?"

"Sure, let's go!"

They both got in Spencer's Camaro and headed back to the gas station. Once they arrived, they picked a meeting spot for the following day.

* * *

Out on the street, it was 7:55 p.m. and the sun was just going down. It was a beautiful night. Unfortunately, it was ruined by the constant flow of crackheads. At about 8:00 p.m., Ham started looking for Tina. Finally, she showed up . . . about 10 minutes late.

"Sorry I'm late, daddy," she said.

"It's all good. Just don't be late again."

"I won't."

Taking a closer look at her, he noticed her fat lip and swelling on her left cheek.

"What the hell happened to you?" he asked.

"It's nothing!"

"Yes, it is something! Now tell me who did it."

"It's my dad. He was hitting my mom, and I stepped in the way."

"Where is he right now?"

"At home."

"Let's go," he said.

"Go where?" she asked, in a scared voice.

"To your house."

"Why?"

"So I can teach him not to hit girls."

"Please don't. It will only make things worse."

"Well, just tell me where you live."

After showing him her house, they headed back to Ham's apartment. He rolled a joint and started smoking it. Then he passed it to Tina.

"I need something stronger, daddy," she said.

"Here is a 20. Go do your thing in the bathroom and then come back.

"Yes, daddy!" she said, as she hurried to the bedroom.

He started plotting in his head how he was going to torture her dad. While she was in the bathroom, he took off all his clothes and lay back on the bed. She finally came back into the bedroom.

"Strip! Very slowly," he said.

"Yes, daddy!" she answered. She started to slowly undress for him.

Damn, she looks good, he thought.

"You look good enough to eat!"

She blushed and then pulled off her bra, letting her breasts loose.

"Come over here!" he ordered.

She walked over and sat down next to him on the bed.

"He pulled her on top of him and started kissing her. Her mouth tasted good as if she just brushed her teeth.

"Here, lay down."

After lying down, he started to finger-fucker her, while he left a trail of kisses from her moth to her pussy. While still finger-fucking her, he started to lick her pussy and suck on her clit.

"How's that feel, baby?" he asked.

"Oh my God! So good!"

"Never had your pussy ate before?" he asked.

"Never . . . !" she gasped.

"Well, lay back and enjoy!" he said, as he went back to sucking on her clit while still finger-fucking her.

"Oh shit! I'm ready to cummmmm!" she screamed, as she released all over his hands and face. Then he slid up to kiss her and to slide his hard cock into her tight wet pussy. She cried out as he slid in her. Her cries, gasps, and noises totally turned him on. Before long, he was cumming inside her pussy.

* * *

Getting started early, Smooth showered, shaved, and got dressed. For breakfast, he had a few Pop Tarts. After eating, he picked up the phone and called Miranda.

"Yes, Smooth!" she answered.

"What the fuck! You a mind reader or something?"

"No! It's caller I.D. You should try it sometime."

"Yeah, I should. I got a bad habit of just answering without checking the display."

"So, what's up?" she asked.

"Figured I'd call and see if ya wanted me to take Zorro off your hands."

"He's good here. But if you want to, that's cool."

"Guess I'll leave him with you another day. Which is good, 'cause I got a big day ahead of me."

"Alright. Call me later."

"I will," he said, as he ended the call.

Going into the walk-in closet, he grabbed two black backpacks. If anyone ever looked, they'd wonder why anyone would have this many backpacks. He had them in his bedroom, his truck, at the trap house . . . everywhere. Pulling out his phone, he dialed another number.

"Yellow!' Banga answered.

"Hey, it's me. Where you at?"

"At a girl's house. Why? What's up?"

"I want to meet ya and give you some of these things."

"Okay."

"How many you need?" Smooth asked.

"Four or five would be nice."

"Well, how 'bout I give you six?"

"That'd be plenty."

"Then six it is. Meet me at our old hangout in one hour."

"I'll be there."

Smooth ended the call and put six keys in one bag and 10 in another.

He dialed another number.

"Ya mon?" Stone answered.

"Hey, it's Smooth."

"Waz up, mon?"

"Wanted to see how you looking on product."

"Really low. Waz gon' call ya tomorrow, mon."

"Well, how many ya need?"

"Tin will be fin."

"Alright. Same spot at noon, okay?"

"Okay, mon."

Smooth ended the call, grabbed both bags, and headed out to his truck.

"Once at the spot, Smooth saw Banga leaning up against his car eating a hamburger.

"What's good, my nigga?" Banga asked.

"You see it, bro!"

"Feels good to be back home. Spent all day yesterday with my mom. Felt really good. I definitely got to spend more time here and with my mom."

"Just be glad you got a mom. You could have grown up with a crackhead mom like I did."

"You're right, bro! I thank God for my mom!"

"Well, I got a tight schedule today so I got to go. But call me tonight," Smooth said, as he handed Banga a backpack and returned to his truck.

"Don't forget to call," Smooth said through the open window as he pulled away.

He then headed to meet Stone at the gas station. Once he arrived, Smooth saw Stone sitting on the trunk of his car. Looking around, Smooth didn't see anything out of place, so he circled the block and then pulled in next to Stone. Getting out of the truck, Smooth grabbed a backpack and handed it to Stone.

"Here man!" Stone said, as he handed another backpack to Smooth.

Now it was time to get the rest of his day together, so Smooth called Spencer.

"Hello?" Spencer answered.

"It's me. Where do you want to meet?"

"You remember where the warehouse is?"

"Yes."

"Well, let's meet there then."

"Okay."

After arriving at the warehouse, Smooth called Spencer again.

"Yeah?"

"I'm outside."

"Alright. Put on in," Spencer said, as the big doors opened. Smooth pulled in behind Spencer's Camaro, which was next to a white van. Once Smooth got out of his car, Spencer walked over to the side of the van.

"What's good?" Smooth asked.

"Not much. You ready to do this?"

"Hell yeah! Been ready!"

175

"We will take this van then."

They both got in the van and headed to Rob's apartment. When they arrived, Spencer handed Smooth a dark gun.

"Just shoot him or anyone else with this."

"What is it?"

"It's a tranquilizer. It will knock out a person almost instantly. Just be sure you don't shoot me."

"What? You said shoot you?" Smooth joked.

Getting out of the van, they looked around and hid the dart guns under their shirts. Once they were in front of Rob's apartment, they pulled out the guns and knocked on the door. A few seconds later, the door opened with a young woman standing there. They quickly shot her with a tranquilizer dart and ran through the open door and into the hallway.

"Who is it, baby?" Rob called out.

"It's your worst nightmare, dickhead!" Smooth yelled, as he stepped into the living room.

As soon as he spotted Smooth, Rob tried to reach for a gun on the table, but Smooth and Spencer hit him multiple darts.

"Let's pull the girl all the way in and then you go and back the van in," Smooth said. He pulled the girl in while Spencer backed the van up to the building. He then came around and both of them lifted Rob up and threw him in back. They then got in the van and headed back to the warehouse. As the big doors opened, they pulled in and the lights came on by themselves.

"How do the lights come on?" Smooth asked.

"The doors, lights, alarms, and everything else are connected to my phone."

"That's totally cool! Got to get me a Bat Cave like that!"

"Takes a lot of work. See that thing that looks like a building."

"Yeah!"

"It's a two-bedroom apartment. Completely soundproof."

"Yeah, I got to get me one," Smooth said.

"Alright. Let's get this sucker up!"

They pulled Rob out of the van, chained his hands together, and then hooked him onto the cherry picker. They raised him high enough so his feet were just above the floor. Spencer then handed a pair of scissors to Smooth.

"Your turn."

Smooth cut off Rob's clothes, looked at Spencer, and then asked, "Now what?"

"Now we wait 'til he wakes up."

When Rob finally came awake and realized that he was naked and hanging, panic took over real fast.

"Glad you could join us, Sleeping Beauty!" Spencer said.

"Fuck you!" Rob said.

"Okay. I tried to be nice. I was going to kill you fast. But now I'm gonna make it nice and slow. You're gonna learn what pain is," Spencer said.

Spencer walked over to the table, grabbed a portable torch, and fired it up. He walked over and held it under Rob's armpit. Instantly, Rob's upper arm was covered in third-degree burns. His screams sounded good to Smooth, since he was one of the men who took Rebecca away from him. Spencer then grabbed a filet knife and slowly began to skin Rob like a deer, from his knee to the ankle. He then did the other leg. Rob's screams could probably be heard for miles, if it weren't for the soundproofed building.

Spencer looked back at Smooth and asked, "You want to join me?"

"Sure!" Smooth said, as Spencer handed him the bloody knife.

Smooth stepped up and sliced off Rob's left ear. He then sliced off his right ear. Noticing that Rob kept his eyes closed, Smooth grabbed an eyelid and cut it off, so he could no longer close it.

"I like that!" Spencer said.

"Wish there was more I could do to him!"

"Yeah, me too!"

"You ready to put him out of his misery?" Spencer asked.

"Yes!" Smooth said, as he pulled out his gun and shot Rob in the head.

"Now, step over here so you can wash the blood off your hands."

Smooth walked over and used the hose to clean up.

"Well, we got them both, which is good. But it still don't make it feel better."

"I know what ya mean," Spencer agreed.

TWENTY-FOUR

Getting back to the dorm, China got in line for the phone.

"Hey China, wanna play skin?" another black girl asked.

"Nah, I'm good. I gotta get on the phone."

"Let me know if you change your mind," the girl said.

While waiting for the phone, China watched TV. The news was on. Another school shooting.

"Damn! These motherfuckers are going crazy out there!" China said to another girl.

"Yeah. It's the second one this month. But this one was the worst."

"It's sad, but we're safer in prison. I mean these dudes shot up beauty salons, gas stations, the mall, grocery stores, the post office, schools, churches, and movie theaters. I mean, damn, nowhere out there is safe! Don't get me wrong, prisons are not safe. You're liable to get jumped or stabbed, but it's crazy out there!"

"I know what you mean. And you're right! It's sad that little kids are not even safe at school," she agreed.

"Do you have any kids?" the girl asked.

"No, but I'd like to have some one of these days."

"I got three and I worry about them every day. Just lucky that I get to call them every night and see them every weekend."

"Yeah. I'd say you're very lucky. How much time you got left?" China asked.

"I got about four months left."

"That's not that long. Hopefully, you can stay out of trouble so you don't come back."

"Don't worry. I'm not coming back. This trip definitely cured me. Not coming back. No sir-ee!"

"China, you're up for the phone," someone hollered.

Grabbing the phone, China dialed Smooth's number.

"Please say your name after the beep," the automated voice asked.

Beep!

"China."

"Please hold while your call is connected."

Ring, ring, ring, ring, ring, ring!

This call may be recorded and monitored. Thank you for using G.T.L.

"China?" Smooth asked.

"Yeah, it's me, baby! Who'd you think it was?"

"You. It's just you never call this early. Is something wrong?" Smooth asked.

"No! Nothing's wrong, but I got some good news."

"What is it?" he asked.

"They are transferring me to Loxahatchee work camp."

"And that's good?" Smooth asked.

"Yeah, it's a little closer to home, but the main thing is I'll have more freedom and a good job, and they say it's really laid back."

"As long as you like it, that's all that matters."

"Well, I won't know 'til I get there. But I'm super excited."

"I can tell."

"So, how's everything with you?" she asked.

"Good. Can't complain. Business is really good."

"Seen Roxy or GaGa?"

"Seen them both last night, when I ate at Roxy's. Said they gonna see you next weekend."

"Next weekend?" she asked.

"Yes, but don't worry, I'll be there this weekend, babe."

"I can't wait to see you."

"Me either. I miss you so much," Smooth told her.

"How's Zorro?"

"He's getting really big. But he acts like a puppy. He jumps all over everyone and tries to get everyone to pick him up or pet him."

"Thank you for all the pictures."

"You're welcome. I'm gonna take some more for ya, too."

"I love you, and I feel so lucky to have you."

"I love you too; and whether you like it or not, you're stuck with me for life," he joked.

You have one minute left, said the automated voice.

"Alright. I love you and will talk to you tomorrow."

"I love you, too," China said.

* * *

It was 7:45 p.m. Almost time to head back home, Ham thought, which was good because he only had a $10 and $20 piece left. Looking back, Ham spotted a cop car pull around the corner. He took off walking, trying not to run or get the police's attention. But it looked like they were coming for him. He pulled out the 20 and swallowed it. And just as he was ready to throw the 10 piece out, the cop car sped up and cut him off. The officer in the passenger side got out and Ham made a run for it. As soon as he turned the corner, he threw his gun away in some bushes. Luckily, the cop didn't see. But when he turned another corner, there was another cop there with his gun out.

"Freeze, nigger!" the cop yelled.

Not wanting to give them a reason, he stopped and put his hands up. Ham waited until they told him to move.

"Get down on the ground," the officer ordered. Ham got on the ground. The officer put his knee into Ham's back as he cuffed him. He grabbed him roughly by the arm and pulled him up. He then slammed him against the side of the cop car.

"Why'd you run, dumbass?" an officer asked.

"'Cause I just bought a dime piece."

"What else you got?"

"Nothing man. I swear!"

"You got anything sharp that will cut me or poke me?"

"No, sir," Ham replied.

The officer had Ham bend over the back of the police car, while he emptied his pockets.

"So, what were you gonna do with this?" the officer asked, holding up the dime piece.

"I was gonna smoke it."

"Well, not tonight, 'cause your dumb black ass is going straight to jail. Pass go, but do not collect $200," the officer joked, as he put Ham in the back of the car.

As the car pulled away, he saw Tina. He hoped she would be okay until he got out. It would be really nice to get her off of drugs—period. Ham wondered how she was going to get drugs now that he would be gone for a few days or longer. He couldn't imagine her selling her body to someone else. He shouldn't care, but he did. Once they arrived at Martin County Jail, Ham was booked.

"Hands right here. Don't move them," Officer Lebowitz ordered. "Alright, come this way. Now to fingerprint you. Put your hands here."

About 10 minutes later, they took him into a 4-Zone One. As soon as he got in, he put his stuff in his room and went to the phone. Luckily, one was open, so he grabbed it and called Meka. After going through all the automated prompts, Meka came on the line.

"Boy, what'd you do?" she asked.

"I got caught slipping, but I only got caught with one dime piece. So it's only possession of crack cocaine."

"So, you didn't get caught with your gun?"

"I told you, I only got caught with a dime piece."

"So, what's your bond?"

"Won't know until I go to first appearance tomorrow, but it shouldn't be much."

"Let me know as soon as you can, and I'll bond your ass out. In the meantime, don't drop the soap."

"Very funny! I'm gonna go so I can call Banga."

"Alright. Call me when you get your bond."

After hanging up with Meka, Ham called Banga. Once the automated prompts were done, Banga came on the line.

"Yello?" Banga asked.

"Bro, it's me! I just got busted."

"How bad?" Banga asked.

"All they got on me was a dime piece, so it's only possession of crack cocaine. I was able to ditch my toast and the rest."

"That's good. Have you got a bond yet?"

"No. Won't get that until I go to first appearance tomorrow."

"Where you at in there?"

"A 4-Zone One."

"Alright, I got a real homeboy in there. His name is Jacob Spears, but everyone calls him Kentucky. Get with him, and tell him you're my cousin. And if you need anything, just ask him. And tell him to call me tonight."

"I will."

"Alright. Let me get back to work."

"Later, bro!"

After hanging up, Ham headed back to his room to make his bed and meet his cellmate. When he got to his room, there was a white dude with a Mohawk and real nice, badass tattoos. He was sitting at the table and writing.

"Here, let me get out of your way," the guy said.

"Nah, man. That's good. You cool, right where you are."

"Well, my name's Kentucky."

"Ha-ha!" Ham burst out laughing.

"What's so funny?"

"Oh sorry. See, I just got off the phone with my cousin and he told me to hook up with you, and now we are roommates."

"Who's your cousin?"

"Banga!"

"Yeah, that's my dawg," Kentucky said.

"He told me to tell you to call him tonight."

"I will. So, you his cousin for real?"

"Yeah."

"How's he doing?"

"He's doing good. Right now he's in Miami visiting his mother."

"That's good."

"Damn man, what time they feed around here?"

"Shit, they just fed us three hours ago. Next meal is breakfast at 5:30 a.m. Why?"

"'Cause I'm starving. I was just fixing to go eat when they busted me."

"I got something for ya," Kentucky said, as he pulled out a big bag of food from the bunk.

"Here ya go. It's not much, but it will do," he said, as he handed Ham a bag of barbeque chips and a pack of chocolate cream cookies.

"Thanks man!" Ham said, as he took the food.

"You drink coffee?" Kentucky asked.

"Yeah, why?"

"Here, I'll make us both a cup."

Kentucky pulled out an orange bag of Billy Brew instant coffee He made two cups and handed one over to Ham.

"I really appreciate it."

"It's the least I can do."

ONE YEAR LATER

"So, how does it feel?" one of China's friends at the work camp asked.

"It feels real good. Can't get here fast enough. These three years have gone by really slowly."

"I feel you. This is my third time in prison and hopefully my last time."

"I don't understand it. If you hate it here and don't want to come back, then why do you keep doing stuff to come back?"

"I got two kids, and it's hard to raise them and feed them. Do you know how hard it is to keep food on the table for them? With a legal job? Impossible!"

"I don't know how it feels, thankfully!" China said.

"Yeah, not all of us were born with a silver spoon up our ass!"

"Hold on now! I grew up poor in the projects! Sometimes we only had rice for dinner. My mother raised us herself while working two jobs. My boyfriend and I went through a lot to get where we are. I know not everyone is lucky. I understand that. But believe me, I know what it's like to go hungry, and I know what it's like growing up poor."

"You're right! It's just you got it good, and we can't help but be jealous. You got a good family, good boyfriend, and full draw every week."

"Well, I'll tell you what. You two write introduction letters tonight and I'll mail them to my man and have him hook you up with some of his friends," China said.

"For real?" Tabby asked.

"Yeah? Think he'd really be able to hook us up?" Jane asked.

"Hell yeah! He will hook you up. Make sure you give me the letters tonight so I can mail them. I'm gonna leave you two my number so you all can reach me. Maybe we will all hook up in Miami."

"Hell yeah! I've never been to Miami."

"Me either. I've never been anywhere except here and Orlando."

"I'll show you two how to really party."

"Alright, ladies. Lunch break is over. Back to work," a guard said.

China stood up and threw her trash in the bag she had been carrying for the past year in the outside work program. She loved it. She left in the morning at 7:00 a.m. and came back around 4:00 p.m. Her group walked the streets and collected trash. After being locked up inside the gates, it was nice to go outside every day and get fresh air.

"So, what do you think of that new Officer Tompkins?" Jane asked.

"He's okay. But he is nothing compared to Smooth," China said proudly.

"Shit! I hope he's got some hot friends, girl. I haven't had dick in six years. And I only got one month left. I don't care who he is, but it'd be nice if he were hot! Know what I mean?" Jane said.

"Yeah, I know what you mean. As soon as Smooth picks me up, we going straight to the motel room. And second somewhere to eat!"

"You sound like you got your ducks all lined up."

"Me?"

"Yes, you! Hell, I don't know where I'm going. I don't have anywhere to live, so I'll probably be at the nearest shelter or Salvation Army."

"You serious?" China asked, as she picked up a Coke can and put it in her bag.

"Dead serious!"

"Well, I might be able to help you. Smooth owns a couple apartments, so maybe he'll have an extra room. I'll definitely ask tonight while I'm on the phone."

"That'd be really helpful. But I don't want to be a burden."

"Nah, I got ya, girl."

"I'm gonna hold you to your word," Jane said.

"God, I still can't believe I get out in like six days."

"I'm happy for you."

* * *

"Hey man! Can I get a 20 piece?" a crackhead asked.

"Yeah, man. Here!" Ham took the $20 and handed the man his piece.

"Hey there!" he heard a sexy voice. Ham turned around and saw a woman. He could tell she used to be beautiful, but the crack turned her out.

"What can I do for you?" Ham asked.

"I got this ring for a 50 piece!" she said.

"Let me see it," Ham said, as he grabbed it. It was nice and it looked real. "I'll tell ya what. I'll give you two 20 pieces."

"Okay, that will do," she said, as he gave her the two 20s.

As soon as she got the crack, she disappeared, running off to a flophouse to smoke or shoot it up.

Ham's mind went to Tina. After he got out of jail, he went to her house to let her know he was out. They kept seeing each other and having sex. She basically lived with him. They started talking about how they wanted a family and with kids.

One night, about three months ago, she told him, "I'm done! No more drugs for me!"

The first two weeks was torture, but she got over the detox. He was so proud of her. Then he got her going to classes to prepare for her GED. She had totally turned her life around 100%. She put on a little bit of weight, but all in the right spots . . . her tits and ass.

It was almost 8:00 p.m., the end of his day. Right on time, Tina showed up and said, "Hey daddy!" she said, giving him a kiss.

"Hey baby!"

"You ready to go home?" she asked.

"Yeah, let's go," he said, as he took her hand and they started walking back to the apartment.

"So, how was your day?" she asked.

"Same as usual out here."

"I'm glad I got myself back on track. I don't know what in the hell made me start that shit, but I'm glad I did start."

"Why are you glad?" he asked confused.

"Because if I didn't start, I never would have met you . . . and you're one of the best things to happen to me. You know what they say: Everything happens for a reason."

"You're right about that!" he said, as they reached the apartment and headed straight to his bedroom.

"Okay, now I want you to sit down," she said.

"Why?" he asked.

"Just sit down."

He did as he was asked.

"Guess what?"

"What?" he asked.

"I'm pregnant!"

"You mean I'm gonna be a father?" he asked with great excitement.

"Yep! You're going to have a kid."

An idea popped into his head.

"Sit down," he said.

"Why?"

"Just sit down."

When she sat down, he reached into his pocket, pulled out a ring, and got down on his knee.

"Tina! You're gonna be my baby's mom. Well, I want you to be more. So, Tina, will ya marry me?"

"Yes!" she screamed, as the both jumped up and hugged, with tears of joy running down their faces.

TWENTY-FIVE

With a long day ahead of him, Smooth got out of bed, showered, dressed, and took Zorro to Miranda's. He was leaving the next day to go out of town to pick up China. He was so excited. She was all that he thought about. He couldn't wait to wrap his hands around her.

He swung by Amanda's. As she opened the door, she said, "Hey there, sexy!"

"Hey!"

Amanda closed the door and led the way to the kitchen. Once there, he put the backpack on the table.

"Here are six more of those things I need cooked up. No rush! I'll take the four you got now."

"No rush?" she asked.

"No, because I'll be out of town for a few days. These four will last them until then."

"Okay. Whatever you say, boss!" she joked.

"Sorry, but I gotta run. I'm late. I'll see you when I get back in town."

After leaving Amanda's, Smooth headed to the trap house and was happy to see Sue's Caprice and Guru's Charger out in front. When he opened the door, he saw both of them playing video games and smoking a blunt.

"Hey guys!"

"Hey Smooth," Guru said.

"What's up, Smooth?" Sue asked.

Here are four keys. Should last you 'til I get back. I'll only be gone for two days," Smooth told them.

"Yeah, four should be plenty," Sue agreed.

"Alright. I'm outta here."

"Later, Smooth," Sue called.

Back in the truck, Smooth had to make just one more stop. Then he could leave for Loxahatchee in the morning to pick up China.

As he pulled up to the gas station, he didn't see Stone, so he pulled into the parking lot to wait. While he was flipping through stations on the radio, a movement caught his eye. As he turned he head to see, two guys pointed guns at him. Before he could even react, they opened fire. Smooth felt every shot, as pain seared every part of his body. Blood flew all over the seat and windshield. His last thought was of China.

TO BE CONTINUED

BOOKS BY GOOD2GO AUTHORS

GOOD 2 GO FILMS PRESENTS

**THE HAND I WAS DEALT- FREE WEB SERIES
NOW AVAILABLE ON YOUTUBE!
YOUTUBE.COM/SILKWHITE212**

SEASON TWO NOW AVAILABLE

To order books, please fill out the order form below:

To order films please go to www.good2gofilms.com

Name:_____

Address:_____

City: _____ State: _____ Zip Code: _____

Phone:_____

Email:_____

Method of Payment: Check   VISA   MASTERCARD

Credit Card#:_____

Name as it appears on card: _____

Signature: _____

Item Name	Price	Qty	Amount
48 Hours to Die – Silk White	$14.99		
Business Is Business – Silk White	$14.99		
Business Is Business 2 – Silk White	$14.99		
Business Is Business 3 – Silk White	$14.99		
Childhood Sweethearts – Jacob Spears	$14.99		
Childhood Sweethearts 2 – Jacob Spears	$14.99		
Childhood Sweethearts 3 - Jacob Spears	$14.99		
Flipping Numbers – Ernest Morris	$14.99		
Flipping Numbers 2 – Ernest Morris	$14.99		
He Loves Me, He Loves You Not - Mychea	$14.99		
He Loves Me, He Loves You Not 2 - Mychea	$14.99		
He Loves Me, He Loves You Not 3 - Mychea	$14.99		
He Loves Me, He Loves You Not 4 – Mychea	$14.99		
He Loves Me, He Loves You Not 5 – Mychea	$14.99		
Lost and Turned Out – Ernest Morris	$14.99		
Married To Da Streets – Silk White	$14.99		
M.E.R.C. - Make Every Rep Count Health and Fitness	$14.99		
My Besties – Asia Hill	$14.99		
My Besties 2 – Asia Hill	$14.99		
My Besties 3 – Asia Hill	$14.99		
My Besties 4 – Asia Hill	$14.99		
My Boyfriend's Wife - Mychea	$14.99		
My Boyfriend's Wife 2 – Mychea	$14.99		
Never Be The Same – Silk White	$14.99		
Stranded – Silk White	$14.99		
Slumped – Jason Brent	$14.99		
Tears of a Hustler - Silk White	$14.99		
Tears of a Hustler 2 - Silk White	$14.99		
Tears of a Hustler 3 - Silk White	$14.99		
Tears of a Hustler 4- Silk White	$14.99		

Tears of a Hustler 5 – Silk White	$14.99		
Tears of a Hustler 6 – Silk White	$14.99		
The Panty Ripper - Reality Way	$14.99		
The Panty Ripper 3 – Reality Way	$14.99		
The Teflon Queen – Silk White	$14.99		
The Teflon Queen 2 – Silk White	$14.99		
The Teflon Queen 3 – Silk White	$14.99		
The Teflon Queen 4 – Silk White	$14.99		
The Teflon Queen 5 – Silk White	$14.99		
The Teflon Queen 6 - Silk White	$14.99		
Tied To A Boss - J.L. Rose	$14.99		
Tied To A Boss 2 - J.L. Rose	$14.99		
Time Is Money - Silk White	$14.99		
Young Goonz – Reality Way	$14.99		
Subtotal:			
Tax:			
Shipping (Free) U.S. Media Mail:			
Total:			

Make Checks Payable To:
Good2Go Publishing
7311 W Glass Lane,
Laveen, AZ 85339

35674056712210

CPSIA information can be obtained at www.ICGtesting.com
Printed in the USA
LVOW10s1449071016

507864LV00013B/438/P